D1187242

DOCTOR · WHO

Wetworld

Also available in the Doctor Who *series:*

STING OF THE ZYGONS
Stephen Cole

THE LAST DODO
Jacqueline Rayner

WOODEN HEART
Martin Day

FOREVER AUTUMN
Mark Morris

SICK BUILDING
Paul Magrs

DOCTOR·WHO

Wetworld

MARK MICHALOWSKI

BBC
BOOKS

2 4 6 8 10 9 7 5 3

Published in 2007 by BBC Books, an imprint of Ebury Publishing.
Ebury Publishing is a division of the Random House Group Ltd.

© Mark Michalowski, 2007

Mark Michalowski has asserted his right to be identified as the author of
this Work in accordance with the Copyright, Design and Patents Act 1988.

Doctor Who is a BBC Wales production for BBC One
Executive Producers: Russell T Davies and Julie Gardner
Series Producer: Phil Collinson

Original series broadcast on BBC Television. Format © BBC 1963.
'Doctor Who', 'TARDIS' and the Doctor Who logo are trademarks of the
British Broadcasting Corporation and are used under licence.

The Random House Group Ltd Reg. No. 954009.
Addresses for companies within the Random House Group can be found
at www.randomhouse.co.uk.

A CIP catalogue record for this book is available from the British Library.

ISBN 978 1 84607 271 0

The Random House Group Ltd makes every effort to ensure that the
papers used in our books are made from trees that have been legally
sourced from well-managed credibly certified forests. Our paper
procurement policy can be found at www.randomhouse.co.uk.

Series Consultant: Justin Richards
Project Editor: Steve Tribe
Cover design by Lee Binding © BBC 2007

Typeset in Albertina and Deviant Strain
Printed and bound in Germany by GGP Media GmbH

For my sister, Julie

High above the still waters of the swamp, the bird carved out spirals in the purple sky, sharp eyes constantly on the lookout for lunch. Warm air rising from the water caught under her steel-blue wings, lifting her higher and higher towards the bloated orange sun.

Suddenly, down in the swamp below, something caught her eye: a tiny flicker of motion on the mirror-smooth surface. Silently, and with only hunger in her mind, she pulled in her wings and dropped like a stone. At the last moment, honed by years of instinct and experience, she stretched out her wings to slow her fall. Just metres from the water, she opened her beak, ready to gulp down the fish that she could see.

And then a glossy tentacle flicked out of the water, wrapped itself around her neck, and dragged her under.

The heavy silence of the swamp was broken momentarily by the thrashing of wings and a frantic splashing as she vanished. All that was left was a little froth of bubbles and a set of slowly decaying ripples, spreading out across the waters of the swamp. It was over in less than a second.

And then there was just the sun, beating down, and the wetness and the silence.

ONE

'So,' said Martha Jones, folding her arms.

She leaned against the handrail that ran around the central console of the time machine.

'Flying the TARDIS. What's all that about, then?'

From beneath her feet, muffled by the grating on which she stood and the weird-looking electronic tool held in his mouth, the Doctor said: 'Mphhhpphh... mmm... mppppffhfhf.'

Martha nodded wisely.

'That's all well and good,' she said. 'But it doesn't really answer my question, does it?'

She dropped, cat-like, to her knees and pressed her face against the floor, squinting to see exactly what the Doctor was doing, down in the bowels of the TARDIS.

'I said—'

'I heard what you said!' snapped back the Doctor, yanking the thing out of his mouth with a scowl. 'But what you don't understand is—'

And he shoved it back between his teeth and mphphphed a bit more, this time with added emphasis, until Martha shook her head exasperatedly and stood up. She wandered around the console, covered with what looked like the contents of a particularly poor car boot sale. There were brass switches, a bicycle pump and something that looked like one of those paperweights with bubbles in it. She was wondering exactly what any of these weird objects had to do with flying through time and space when she suddenly found the Doctor standing in front of her, sonic screwdriver in hand, his hair all ruffled and askew.

'Well?'

'Um… yeah,' replied Martha cagily, wondering what he was on about. 'Probably.'

'Good!'

And he was off, racing past her, around to the other side of the console, where he grabbed the paperweight and gave it a delicate tweak. All around her, the subtle burblings and electronic grumblings of the TARDIS changed key ever so slightly, settling into something much more comfortable. Martha followed him, watching as he fiddled and faddled with the junk set into the console's luminous green surface.

'What I was saying before…' she ventured, watching his narrowed eyes.

'Yes,' he said, nodding firmly. 'Croissants. For breakfast. Definitely. We'll pop over to Cannes and pick a—'

'Not the croissants,' she interrupted.

'No problem. Porridge is fine by me. Edinburgh – 1807. Fine vintage.'

'I'm not talking about breakfast.'

He jolted upright, as if he'd received an electric shock, and turned to her, eyes wide and manic.

'You mean it's *lunchtime?*' He glanced at his watch, frowned, shook it and then placed it to his ear. 'Why didn't you tell me?' He rolled his eyes and slipped the sonic screwdriver into the breast pocket of his dark-brown suit. 'I've been down there for *hours.*'

'You've been down there for fifteen minutes.'

He opened his mouth to say something, but quick as lightning Martha clamped her hand over it.

'What I'm trying to tell you,' she said with slow and forced patience, taking her hand away. 'What I've been trying to tell you for three days now, is that you ought to let me know how the TARDIS works – and if not how it actually works, how it *operates.* How *you* operate it.'

She ignored the muffled protestations and the wiggled eyebrows. 'I mean – all I want is some basic lessons, yeah? Just "Press this button to get us out of danger; press *this* button to sound an alarm; press *that* button to get BBC Three." That kind of thing.'

Martha folded her arms again and leaned back against the console, putting on her most reasonable voice. 'Now that's not too much to ask, is it? And it would help you too – you wouldn't have to be hovering over this thing twenty-four seven.' She patted the console behind her.

The Doctor puckered up his lips thoughtfully, reached into his pocket, pulled out the sonic screwdriver and shoved it back in his mouth.

'Mpfhphfhhff,' he said.

She reached out and pulled the device from him, extracting an indignant *Ooof!* along with it.

'You think I'm too thick, don't you!'

He just stared at her – actually, he just stared at the sonic screwdriver. Martha looked down at it, hanging between her fingertips, and pulled a face at the dribble on it before handing it gingerly back to him. She pointed at her own chest with her free hand.

'Medical student, remember?' she said. 'A levels.'

The Doctor raised an eyebrow.

'Driving licence,' she added.

The other eyebrow joined the first one.

'Martha, Martha, Martha,' he said patronisingly, making her instantly want to slap him. 'Operating the TARDIS isn't about intelligence. It's not about pressing this button, then pulling that lever. It's much more difficult than that.' He reached out and stroked the curved, ceramic edge of the console. 'It's about intuition and imagination; it's about *feeling* your way through the Time Vortex.'

'It's about kicking it when it doesn't work, is what it's about.'

He pulled a hurt little boy face.

'Don't start that,' she warned, a smile twitching the corner of her mouth upwards. 'I've heard you, when you think I'm not around, stomping and banging the console.'

'Well there you go then!' he said triumphantly, as if that settled the matter. 'It's about stomping and *banging* your way through the Time Vortex!'

He turned away, stowing the sonic screwdriver back in his pocket (after, Martha noted with a grimace, wiping it clean on the sleeve of his jacket again).

'Intelligence is overrated, Martha – believe you me. I'd take an ounce of heart over a bucketful of brains any day.'

'Oooh!' mocked Martha. 'Bet you're a whizz in the kitchen!'

The Doctor's eyes lit up again. 'And talking about food… who's up for breakfast? All that talk of croissants is makin' me *mighty* hungry.' He stretched out his right hand. 'And this here hand is a *butterin'* hand! How d'you fancy breakfast at *Tiffany's*?'

Martha's mouth dropped open: '*Tiffany's*? You mean *the real Tiffany's*? As in *Breakfast at*?'

'Where else?' the Doctor beamed back, looking extremely pleased with himself.

'Nice one!' said Martha, a huge grin on her face. 'This is the kind of time and space travelling I signed up for! Although,' she added, 'I'm beginning to suspect you've got a bit of a thing about New York, you know.'

And with that, she was gone.

'New York?'

The Doctor stood in the console room, watching Martha vanish in the direction of the TARDIS's wardrobe. A puzzled frown wrinkled his brow. *New York? Why had Martha mentioned New York when he was taking her to* Tiffany's *near the Robot Regent's palace on Arkon?*

'Must have misheard her,' he decided, tapping at the controls on the console and flicking a finger at what Martha would undoubtedly have thought was just a small, brass, one-eyed owl. Blue-green light pulsed up and down the column at the centre of the console and a deep groaning filled the air, settling down as the TARDIS shouldered its way out of the Time Vortex into the real world.

'Perfect,' the Doctor said to himself. 'Textbook landing. Like to see *Martha* manage a landing as textbook perfect as *that!*'

'Ahhh...,' said the Doctor out loud, somewhat surprised at quite how warm, wet and, well, *swampy* Arkon had become since his last visit.

And slippery.

Because as he stepped from the TARDIS, the sole of his foot skidded on a moss-covered root beneath him, and it was only by grabbing onto the TARDIS's doorframe that he managed to stop himself from ending up on the muddy ground.

The air hit him like a huge, damp blanket. He stood there, one foot still inside the TARDIS, the other hovering a cautious six inches from the ground, and wondered what had gone wrong. Arkon should have been a prosperous, advanced, Earth-like world. Right about now, a hot, F-type star should have been beating down on him, and his senses should have been assailed by the smells, sounds and scents of technology run riot.

But, instead, all around him was a languid silence, punctuated by the occasional sound of splashing water. And the only smells were the fusty smells of swamp gas and damp. A *green* smell. He liked green smells – full of vim and vigour and vegetables.

'Ummm…' he added, looking out over the oily water that stretched away from the steeply sloping bank where the TARDIS had plonked itself. At the other side, a couple of hundred metres away, shaggy trees lowered their branches almost to the water, like a floppy fringe. And through the canopy of leaves above him, an orange-red sun blistered the purplish sky.

'This is just a teensy bit wrong,' he said to himself.

Ferreting around in the TARDIS's wardrobe for something ultra-glam and ultra-chic to wear to *Tiffany's* (think *Audrey Hepburn*, she reminded herself, *think Hollywood glamour*), she just knew that the Doctor would be standing in the console room, tapping his foot impatiently. Well he could just wait. It wasn't often that a girl got to do sophistication when travelling with the Doctor. Jeans, her red leather jacket and stout boots had been the order of the day recently, and she wasn't passing up this chance to shine.

She rooted around for a slinky frock and let out a triumphant 'Yes!' when she found a lilac silk dress and some matching elbow-length gloves with pearl cuffs. In seconds, she'd slipped into them and was twirling and preening in front of the mirror. The frock, it had to be said, was a wee bit tight on her. But if she breathed in – and didn't breathe out *too* much – it'd do. Shoes were a bit trickier, but she found a pair of silver strappy sandals that just about fitted.

'Knock 'em dead, girl!' she told herself as, with a final

tweak of her hair, she bounded out of the wardrobe, ready for her disgustingly decadent breakfast. At *Tiffany's*.

The Doctor was tempted to assume that something had gone very wrong with Arkon's sun, and that it had caused a massive change in the planet's ecosystem, turning it from high-tech paradise to swamp world. He was tempted to think that maybe the Arkonides had been messing with solar modifiers and had mutated their star into the orange ball that hung over him. Or that some attacking alien race had done the fiddling for them in an attempt to wipe the Arkonides out.

In fact he was very tempted to think anything except the one thing that really seemed most likely.

He leaned back into the cool interior of the TARDIS.

'Have you been messing with those controls again?' he shouted to Martha. But not quite loudly enough for her to hear. Because of course Martha *hadn't* been messing with the controls. And the Doctor knew it.

He shook his head ruefully and ventured his foot out onto the mossy tree root, snaggled and sprawled out of the bank like a deformed Twiglet.

'Must get those gyroceptors fixed,' he muttered.

Cautiously, he tested the root with his weight, and it held. The slipperiness was more of a problem: he had to hang on to the TARDIS's doorframe as he shifted his weight onto his outstretched foot. Carefully, he brought the other foot out and found a safe-ish place for it. Finally, he leaned onto it.

'There!' he beamed at his own cleverness. 'Wasn't so

difficult, was—'

With all the comedic grace of one of the Chuckle Brothers, the Doctor began to flail his hands around as his left foot started to slip and slide on the root. And as his other foot decided to join in the fun, he began windmilling his arms frantically, jacket flapping around him. Seconds later, as he felt himself begin to fall, he instinctively grabbed for the open doorway to the TARDIS.

Which was a *big* mistake.

The TARDIS might have been a pretty solid, pretty hefty thing, despite its external dimensions. But it was as subject to the same forces of physics – and friction – as he was. And despite the fact that it had squashed the roots underneath it when it had landed, they were still very slippery roots.

It was, thought the Doctor ruefully as his time and space ship began to move, a bit like launching a battleship. Only without a bottle of champagne smashed against the side of it.

With a creak and groan of roots and a deep squelch of mud, the TARDIS began to slide down the bank towards the water, and the Doctor again began to lose his balance. In fact, in accidentally pushing against the TARDIS, not only had he sent it down the natural runway that the roots provided, but he'd pushed himself in the opposite direction.

'Wellingtons!' was the only thing he managed to cry out to Martha as he landed flat on his back in a spray of muddy water. He lifted himself up on his elbows just in time to see his beloved TARDIS pause at the edge of the swamp before it tipped, almost as if it were waving him goodbye. And in majestic slow motion, the blue box keeled over.

There was an almighty splash, drenching the Doctor with warm, silty water, a brief gush of bubbles and a massive wave that spread out across the swamp. And then the TARDIS was gone.

'Wellingtons,' he repeated in a disbelieving whisper. 'Don't forget your Wellingtons, Martha.'

Martha was sure she heard the Doctor shout something. Just seconds after there was a very slight lurch beneath her feet. But it might just have been the TARDIS settling down. Sometimes it did that after it landed, like her granddad, shifting himself in his armchair, getting comfy for *Strictly Come Dancing*.

But when she reached the console room, there was no sign of the Doctor. Martha – wincing slightly as the straps of the sandals cut into her feet – bent down to peer through the floor grille, wondering if the Doctor was doing some more repairs. But there was no sign of him.

'Doctor?' Martha called, straightening up. No answer.

Then she noticed the door: it was ajar. The reason she hadn't noticed it before was that, as far as she could see, it was dark outside. And that couldn't be right, could it? Not if they were going to breakfast. Not unless he'd landed her in the middle of winter at about 7am. In which case, a lilac silk evening gown and strappy sandals might not be the most practical outfit.

Maybe the TARDIS had landed indoors. Or in an alleyway. Yes, she thought, more confidently this time. That must be it. Excitement skipping in her heart again at the thought of the glamorous treat to come, she bounded over to the door.

Only…

It was *wrong*. The darkness outside the TARDIS was decidedly *wrong*. It was as if something flat and dark and watery-looking had been pressed up against the open door. Martha peered closely. Away to one side, she could vaguely see light – dim, murky, brown light. And in the darkness, if she peered really closely, she could see tiny grains, swirling and twisting.

Martha reached out her hand gently – and found herself touching the darkness. Only it wasn't quite solid. There was a bit of give in it, like some sort of transparent rubber membrane. Delicately, she pushed at it, and it stretched away from her. *Weird*. She pulled her hand back and noted how the stretchy surface rebounded, becoming perfectly flat again.

'Doctor!' she called, wondering whether he could even hear her through this strange browny-blackness.

Martha put out her hand to it again, and felt the firm, textureless surface give. Gritting her teeth, she pushed again – and suddenly, her hand and arm were through it. For a moment, she froze, feeling a cool wetness soak through the silk to her skin.

Water, she thought instantly. *It's wa—*

And before she could even complete the thought, something powerful and muscled wrapped itself around her wrist. Her mouth was still open in an unfinished scream as she was dragged into the death-dark waters…

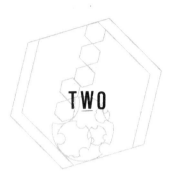

TWO

The Doctor could do nothing but stare blankly at the spot where the TARDIS had vanished. The only thing to mark where she had stood were some scuffed, flattened roots sprouting from the bank.

His first thought had been for Martha – but he suspected that she'd be fine. The fact that just a few air bubbles had broken on the water's surface showed that either the door had closed before it had fallen in, or that the TARDIS had activated its force field. If the entrance to his ship had been completely open, this whole area would have been draining away by now. The cavernous interior of the TARDIS would be soaking up the water like a huge sponge.

But that didn't help him with getting it back.

He needed help. He could try diving down into the lake, but the water looked filthy with mud and silt, and even though – given time – he could probably find it, he wasn't sure he could hold his breath long enough to actually get inside.

Yes, he needed help.

For the first time, he turned his attention properly to his surroundings. What he'd assumed was a river probably wasn't: the water was still and flat. Maybe a lake. The TARDIS had landed on a blunt promontory, sticking out into it. The air was thick with damp although his clothes were starting to dry out a little under the influence of the baleful orange sun. There wasn't much of a breeze, and away in the distance, in the thick trees and bushes behind him and on the other side of the lake, he could hear chirpings and twitterings and rustlings. Twilight was approaching fast, and with it, the Doctor knew, the planet's animals would be coming out to feed.

Get some perspective, he told himself firmly.

And within seconds he'd managed to clamber up one of the nearby trees. Like cupped hands reaching skywards, the branches spread out, thin and silvery, forming a loose, circular cage. Numerous shoots provided plenty of footholds, and soon he was perched precariously in the tree's upper reaches, swaying from side to side as he shifted his weight. A small, grey and red bird twittered and took to the sky, clearly outraged at his intrusion, ignoring his apology.

Clinging on for dear life, he scanned the forest: green, green and more green, broken only by the occasional silver-grey trunk of a taller tree. And, like cracks in crazy paving, zigzags of open darkness where he suspected more rivers or lakes lay.

He narrowed his eyes, and raised his free hand to shelter

them from the sun, now just touching the tops of the trees along the horizon. Wherever he was, it was obviously a planet that spun quickly on its axis. A quick bit of guesstimation put the day's length at no more than twelve hours. So *definitely* not Arkon.

Just a couple of kilometres away, a lazy drift of smoke snaked up into the sky out of the green.

'Seek,' he whispered with a smile, 'and ye shall find…'

Whatever it was, thought the Doctor, wavering unsteadily, it was certainly worth a second look. Overhead, clouds were beginning to gather, obscuring the orangey disc of the moon. Rain was on its way.

'Candy' Kane hated her nickname. Really, really hated it. But like sticky-out ears or goofy teeth, she'd found it impossible to get rid of without some sort of drastic surgery.

Born Candice Margaret Kane to parents who hadn't had the common sense to think ahead and thus save their only daughter from years of torment at the hands of the other kids, Candy had made a fatal mistake. On her first day at school she'd lied that her name was actually Kathryn. A lie she'd been caught out in straight away, which only served to signal to everyone that there was something wrong with 'Candice'. And within days they'd started calling her 'Candy'.

Coming to Sunday had seemed like a good idea – not only would she be starting an exciting, brand-new life, but she'd have the chance to ditch the 'Candy' once and forever. And all at just sixteen! The arrival, three days after planetfall, of a hypermail from her aunt – addressed to 'Candy Kane' – trashed those hopes good and proper.

All of which might well have accounted for the fact that, whenever she could, Candy chose to work on her own. Whether it was scouting along the banks of the lakes and rivers that had drowned the first settlement, looking for washed-up debris, or out hunting for water pigeon eggs, Candy preferred to go it alone. She didn't care that the other settlers thought she was aloof. She *was* aloof. And that was the way she liked it. It was easier to get around quietly on her own. Professor Benson was about the only one she felt happy going out into Sunday's swamps with. Even though she was old enough, Ty Benson didn't pretend to be a mother figure to Candy; she didn't keep asking her 'how she was finding it', or 'how she was fitting in'. She didn't go on about how Candy should make 'more of an effort' to be friendly with the other teenagers. She just let her be, and trusted her to know what she was doing.

Candy adjusted the straps on her backpack, feeling the well-padded water pigeon eggs (all three of 'em!) shift around inside. The size of Earth ostrich eggs, they weren't just a delicacy, but each one could feed a family of four for a day. Food wasn't short for the settlers – the bewildering variety of plants that grew in and around the swamps saw to that. And before the flood they'd had fish galore from the nets that they'd strung up across the river mouths. But it was always a treat to tuck into one of the rich, brown eggs with their double yolks.

She checked her watch and the bloated orb of the sun

as it sank towards the tops of the trees. The thickening clouds were painted orange and purple. Sunday's sunsets were beautiful, but short-lived. Dusk came quickly, and the settlement was a good half-hour away. Candy didn't mind being out after dark: there were few dangerous predators on this part of the planet. Out of the water, at least. Deep in the swamps were a host of unpleasant aquatic beasties, ranging from tiny worms that would bury themselves into your skin, right through to some nasty little fish that had the habit of sinking their razor-sharp teeth into you and refusing to let go, even if you chopped their heads off. And then there were the 'gators – five-metre-long things that were a cross between an alligator and turtle. You really didn't want to be on the wrong end of one of *those*!

But she hadn't seen many of them since the flood. Fish had been in short supply too, which was worrying some of the Sundayans. Anyway, she knew that if she kept away from the water, she'd be fairly safe. The only sizeable animals that travelled through the forest were the otters, and even they didn't tend to move far from water and their nests. And according to Professor Benson they were veggies anyway.

Suddenly, she stopped. Ahead of her, somewhere away over to the right, she heard a noise: it sounded like branches snapping.

Curious – but with the blonde hairs on her arms pricking up into goose bumps – Candy crouched lower behind a fallen tree. Reaching into her backpack, she pulled out her monocular and raised it to her eye, thumbing the switch on the barrel that would bring up the light enhancement.

The blood-lit gloom sprang alive in shades of yellow and ochre. She caught a glimmer of movement, a flexing lemon crescent that rose from the forest floor and swooped up into the canopy. A water pigeon, perhaps. Maybe a curver – or a sea-wader. Candy let out the breath that she didn't know she'd been holding in and stood up. Maybe it was Orlo, blundering around in the forest like he did. A year or so younger than her, Orlo was a big, clumsy lad – quite the opposite of Candy. He was cheerful and good-natured and sometimes went out with her on night-time rambles. But, like Candy, he also enjoyed his own company, and many a time they'd come across each other in the dark, scaring each other in the process.

Candy fished in her backpack and pulled out her torch. Aiming it towards the source of the noises, she flashed out a quick 'Hi!' in Morse code. If it was Orlo, he'd signal back: the two of them had learned Morse code together from an old manual in the *One Small Step*'s shipbrain on the trip to Sunday, just for fun.

Candy peered into the dark, waiting for the reply.

'Hi,' it came back a few seconds later, although the light was colder and more bluish than she remembered Orlo's torch being.

'What's up?' she sent back.

Orlo must have been practising. The reply came back quickly: 'I'm lost.'

Lost? How could he be lost? He knew this bit of the forest as well as she did. Was he winding her up?

'Yeah,' she flashed back. 'You'll be out here all nite then.'

Quick as anything, Orlo sent back: 'That's not how you spell night.' What was he on about?

'What?' she started to send back – but before she could finish the 't', a pale, thin face leaped up out of the bushes just a few yards away, right in the beam of her torch.

'Excuse me,' said the man, his eyebrows raised, 'I think you'll find that correct spelling is the mark of an educated mind.'

Candy stumbled backwards and tripped, smashing her backpack against the trunk of the tree behind her. With a wet crunch, the eggs inside it shattered. She looked up frantically, waving her torch around until it connected with the man's face.

'Or is it the mark of someone with nothing better to do…?' He frowned, shrugged, and stepped out of the bushes into the full glare of her torch. He wore a strange two-piece brown suit, half fastened up the front. His hair was matted with water and dirt, and a daft and slightly scary grin and mad eyes peered out through a mud face-pack. In one hand was something that looked like a metallic pencil. Candy realised that it must have been him that had been signalling to her, and that was his torch.

'Ohhhh,' the man said, raising his free hand. 'Sorry! Not a good habit, that, creeping up on people. I don't know my own stealth, that's my problem.'

He paused and turned the volume control on his smile down from 'manic' to 'friendly'. 'Sorry,' he said again.

'Wh-who—' began Candy.

'Who am I?' The mad grin returned, and Candy took a

step back. The nutter slipped the torch into his pocket and stuck out a grimy hand. Candy glanced down at it, and so did he.

'Oops, sorry,' he apologised again, wiped the hand on his trousers and thrust it out towards her again, dirtier than ever. 'I'm the Doctor.'

Candy just stared at him.

'Ooooo-kaaaaay,' said the man, dropping his hand and backing away slowly. 'I think you'd be happier if I went and stood over *here*.' And he took a dozen paces away from her – and squatted down, wincing a bit at the sogginess of the ground.

'Where are you from?' Candy found herself asking, watching his every move.

'Me? Oh…' The man seemed to consider the question for a moment. 'Just about everywhere, really. Well, that is, apart from *here*. Not from here. Definitely not. Where exactly *is* here, by the way?'

'The Slim Forest,' Candy found herself saying.

'Ah… the Slim Forest. I take it there's a Not-So-Slim Forest around here somewhere then? And maybe a Rather Stocky Forest too? Or has that one been renamed the Big-Boned Forest?'

'What?'

'Sorry – oh, I'm doing it again, aren't I? Sor—'

And then he shook his head as if in frustration at himself.

'It's just that I've lost a friend of mine – back in the swamp. And I'm just the *teensiest* bit eager to find her and make sure she's safe.'

Oh, dear God! thought Candy. *There're two of them.*

'So you see,' continued the man, 'if you could tell me what planet I'm on, I might have some idea of what to expect out there. I mean, I could go through all that "Red sun… narrows it down; point nine Earth normal gravity… narrows it down" malarkey. But it really would be so much easier if you could—'

'Sunday,' Candy interrupted him. 'It's Sunday.'

He narrowed his eyes.

'Sunday the planet?'

Candy nodded.

'Ahhhh!' said the man, springing alarmingly to his feet. 'Never heard of it.' In the ruby gloom, his shoulders sank. 'Looks like it's back to the elimination round, then. Where was I? Oh yes, gravity…'

'How did you get here?'

The man seemed thrown by her sudden question.

'To Sunday? Lovely name for a planet, by the way: the day you arrived? Thank goodness it wasn't Friday – that would have just been silly. Well, my spaceship landed back there. On the edge of the swamp. Before I knew it… *splosh!*' The words were tumbling out of him almost faster than Candy could keep up.

'What about your friend?'

'She was inside the ship. Still is, hopefully.' The man paused, and even in the gloom, his eyes suddenly looked incredibly gentle. Incredibly fragile. 'Please,' he said softly. 'I need help.'

Candy thought for a moment.

'It's too late now – too dark. If your ship's fallen in the swamp, you'll need some serious muscle to get it out.'

'And this serious muscle… Is there some around here? I mean, apart from yourself.' He looked her up and down. Candy found herself grinning.

'We'll have to go back to the settlement. Tell them. Let them decide.'

'Ah… the settlement. That'll be where the smoke's coming from, will it? Well, it's a plan,' the Doctor agreed with a nod. He gestured ahead. 'Ladies first,' he smiled, and then grimaced. 'Ooh, that was *terribly* sexist of me, wasn't it?' And before Candy could take a step, he pushed in front of her.

'Age before beauty,' he called over his shoulder as she set off after him. 'Pot before kettle.'

Behind them, unseen in the darkness, a dozen pairs of eyes watched them go. The final shreds of twilight of the sun caught in them, like the dying embers of a fire, burning softly…

THREE

'**S**o,' said the Doctor after a few minutes of plodding through the darkened forest, illuminated only by the shreds of red moonlight shining through gaps in the clouds. 'Tell me about yourself. What's your name?'

Candy looked sideways at him. He'd kept a few yards from her, clearly aware that she still felt uncomfortable about him.

'Candice Kane,' she said.

'Nice to meet you, Candice Kane.' This time he didn't stick out his muddy hand for her to shake. Both of them were jammed firmly in his trouser pockets. 'So how long have you been on Sunday, Candice?'

'Almost a year,' she said.

'That long, eh? And how many of you are there?'

'Fewer than 400 of us now,' Candy replied, wondering why he was asking. Surely he must know about the flood.

'This settlement,' he went on, gesturing ahead of them. 'Have a name?'

'The old one was called Sunday City – this one'll be the same, once we've got it up and running again.'

'Human imagination,' he said with a grin. 'Never underestimate it. And what year is this?' he asked, before suddenly apologising again. 'I'm sounding like a tourist, aren't I?'

'What *year*?' She looked at him sideways. 'You're not one of those New Julian weirdos that want to go messing with the calendar and everything, are you?'

'Oh no,' the Doctor replied confidently. 'Just space travel, you know: relativity, time dilation. All that stuff.'

'Right,' Candy said slowly. 'Well round here it's the usual 2108.'

'Ah… The First Wave,' he said thoughtfully as if to himself. 'Anyway,' he added briskly, as if he didn't want her thinking about what he'd said, 'you said "up and running again". Problems with the first one?'

Candy took a breath and, knowing that they still had another half-hour's walk to go, told him the story.

The first wave of settlers had come to Sunday just over a year ago, and all 800 of them had set up along the banks of the river, rapidly building quite a decent little town from the prefabricated huts and buildings they'd brought with them. Self-sufficient in almost everything, they anticipated a tough but fair start to their new lives. They had a couple of trucks, a fabricator plant to churn out more construction panels, a generator station. Everything looked like it was going to be fine – they'd have a nice little city up and running for the next wave of colonists.

But then, three months ago, the communications and observation satellite they'd left in orbit detected something disturbing. Sunday's orbit would take it through the debris cloud of a recently destroyed asteroid, smashed to dust when it passed close to one of the system's gas giant planets. The settlers were worried – but when they analysed the data on the asteroid fragments, they relaxed a little: they were all fairly small, none of them large enough to cause an Extinction Level Event. As the planet entered the debris cloud, the Sundayans sat back, watched the skies and hoped for nothing worse than a nice light show.

'And I take it,' the Doctor interrupted, 'that the outcome wasn't good.'

Candy nodded, pushing aside bushes as they squelched through the forest. The soft pattering of rain could be heard.

'Most of the fragments burned up in the atmosphere – it was the best fireworks show we'd ever seen. I mean,' she enthused guiltily, 'really spectacular. These huge fireballs and streaks across the sky. We all stood outdoors and watched. The little kids loved it.'

Candy paused, remembering the light show.

'A couple of pieces got through,' Candy continued. 'They didn't just burn up like all the others. One of them struck the ground a couple of hundred kilometres away – shaking the ground, knocking a few of the half-constructed buildings down. Everyone panicked. People were screaming and crying, but the scientists said we'd be OK – the dust cloud it threw up was tiny, really. Nothing to worry about.' She paused. 'It was the last piece, though. *That* was the problem. The meteorite hit the ocean, just a kilometre or so offshore – about six from Sunday City.' Candy stopped again, remembering that night.

'A tidal wave,' whispered the Doctor, closer to her than he'd been a moment ago. He glanced up at the sky as the rain made the forest around them hiss.

'It just rolled in along the river – a great, black wall, moonlight catching the top edge of it.' Candy shuddered at the memory. 'All we could do was stand and stare at it, you know?' She turned to the Doctor and he was there, just a couple of metres away. 'And then everyone started screaming and running. People were grabbing their kids, grabbing bags, clothes, anything they could. It was chaos. They weren't even all running in the right direction. Some of them headed upslope, away from the river. Others – God knows why! – were running along the bank. Maybe they thought they'd get further by staying on the flat. Some of them…' Candy closed her eyes, but the images in her head played on. 'Some of them just went in their houses, calm as anything, and closed the doors. We managed to meet up on the other side of the hill, after the wave had subsided.' Candy remembered them all gathering around a pathetic fire – dry wood torn from the tops of the salt-trees where the water hadn't reached, the smell of the sap, soapy and pungent at the same time, as it spat and crackled. She remembered the steamy smoke, coiling away into the warm night. Taking their hopes and dreams with it.

There had been people running around, still wailing and

crying, asking if anyone had seen this person or that. She could still see the blank faces of some of the older people who didn't seem to quite realise what had happened. Marj Haddon, her face even paler than usual in the firelight, sitting hugging her knees, wrapped in a soggy old blanket and not even asking about her partner, Lou. The Richlieu twins, asking their grandpa where Mum and Dad were, and the look on their grandpa's tear-stained face as he tried to find a way to tell them…

'We lost almost everything,' Candy said after a few moments. She brushed her straggly blonde hair back from her face, slicking it against her head. The Doctor didn't even seem to notice the rain. 'Some of us went back the next day – to see, you know…' Her mouth was suddenly as dry as leaves.

'The waters had fallen by then – a bit, anyway. Almost everything useful was either underwater or had been washed away. Even the ship was gone. We managed…' She broke off, feeling herself choking up at the memories her tale was bringing up. 'Some of the buildings on the edge of the city had survived, and we managed to salvage a lot of the stuff that had floated to the surface.' Candy had to stop again as her mind raced ahead of her mouth. She looked up into the Doctor's eyes. 'And then we started to find the bodies.'

Candy was suddenly aware that she was sobbing into the warm, muddy shoulder of a complete stranger. A complete stranger who held her whilst she let it all out. She barely noticed as the rain continued to fall.

* * *

She didn't know how long he held her – silently, saying nothing, passing no judgements. No telling her not to cry, no telling her that everything would be alright. No vague, meaningless words of comfort from someone who hadn't been there, someone who hadn't seen what she'd seen. No trying to be a father or a brother or a friend. In a strange way, he reminded her of Ty.

Eventually, she pulled away from him, and he let her.

'Sorry,' she said, rubbing her nose on the back of her hand. The rain was falling heavily now, and it just made her face wetter.

'Don't be silly,' the Doctor said. 'Nothing like a good cry. Lets all those brain chemicals run free, sort themselves out.'

'Does it?' she sniffed.

He stared at her – and shrugged.

'Probably,' he said, as if he'd just made it up. 'But you stuck it out – all of you. You stayed.'

'Not much choice. The *One Small Step* – our ship – was gone. And the second wave of colonists'll be here in a year. Can't let 'em down, can we?'

'Oh no,' agreed the Doctor. 'That'd never do. Sounds like you could do with a bit of moral support.'

Candy snorted a laugh.

'Couldn't we just!'

'Well perhaps you'd better take me to Sunday City – I've got a City & Guilds in moral support.' He beamed the smiliest of smiles. 'First class!'

* * *

'I'm worried about her,' said Col, checking the locks on the cages and throwing the clipboard onto Ty's desk. It narrowly missed her coffee cup, the one with the picture of the kitten with its paws up in the air and the caption saying: 'You'll never take me alive!'

Ty snatched the cup up in an easy, fluid gesture.

'Hey!' she said, her voice deep, but tinged, as always, with just a hint of amusement.

'She'll be fine – Candy knows the Slim Forest like the back of her hand. Anyways up...' He plonked himself in an orange plastic chair across the desk from Ty. 'What's the result of the latest maze test?'

He threw a glance towards the other side of the timber-walled room where twelve cages sat, three rows of four. Each contained an otter – most of them curled up on the dried leaves they gave them for bedding. A couple were sitting back on their haunches, watching the two humans talk about them.

Ty shook her head and ran her fingers through her braided, black hair. She'd been talking about getting it cut for a while, but Col knew that was all it was: talk. Ty was too proud of her braids to let anyone at them with a pair of scissors.

'Same as before: the newer ones are about sixty per cent worse at it than the older ones. I took the three from last week out earlier and let them go: they were beginning to work out how to work the locks. Too clever by half, some of 'em.'

'Sssh!' Col chided her with a grin. 'They might hear you!

Who knows how sensitive they might be? You don't want to hurt their little egos. Not with *those* claws, anyway.'

Ty smiled.

'If you ask me, it's the ones we've caught in the last two days that we have to be nice to.' She raised her voice and directed her words at the cages. 'They're the dim-but-aggressive ones.'

Col turned to look – they were still getting back on track with their research into the otters since the flood had washed away almost everything they'd done before. And they were no closer to working out why the otters seemed to get smarter and smarter the longer they were in captivity.

'Just don't tell Pallister, that's all.' Ty's voice had dropped in volume and in pitch. Col knew what was coming. He rolled his eyes and slid his half-empty cup across the desk. He really didn't want this conversation again.

'I've told you, Pallist—'

'Pallister's an opportunist,' Ty cut in. 'He'd never have been elected Chief Councillor if it hadn't been for the flood. And a right mess-up he's made of the reconstruction.'

'Oh, and you could have done better?'

Ty waved his comment away.

'I'm not saying that. All I'm saying is that he's out to make a name for himself. He's an old-style colonial. Future only knows why they let him come out here. No, scratch that: *I* know why they let him come out here. Because he was a middle-ranking nobody of a technician who had a few organisational skills and knew people in the right places. And with the flood, he's come bobbing to the surface like…'

Her voice tailed off as she realised what she was about to say. 'Anyway, if Pallister gets it into his head the otters are halfway intelligent, he'll have 'em rounded up, chain-ganged and set to work building houses or whatever. It'll be Lucius Prime and the lemurs all over again, and we all know how *that* ended.'

There was a sudden clumping noise outside and the wooden door to the lab was thrown open. Standing there, illuminated by the overhead fluorescents, was Candy, sopping wet. She had a strange look on her face.

'Hiya,' she smiled – but it was a tight, awkward smile.

'What's up, honey?' asked Ty instantly, jumping to her feet.

Without answering, Candy stepped inside. Behind her was someone else – a someone else dressed in a weird, dark-brown two-piece with a couple of buttons down the front, a muddy white undershirt and some sort of tie around his neck. His face was smeared with dirt and his drenched hair was struggling to spring up. He grinned brightly, and it was as though someone had turned on another light.

'Hello!' he said. 'I'm the Doctor. Can I interest you in some uplifting words – cheery banter and rousing speeches a speciality.'

Martha coughed herself awake, choking and retching on the stale water in her throat and lungs.

It was dark. Almost pitch black, in fact. She wasn't cold – which, in her dazed state surprised her somewhat – but she wasn't particularly warm either. She lay still for a few moments, trying to get her bearings, trying to remember what had happened.

The last thing she remembered was pushing her hand out of the TARDIS, through the stretchy force field, or whatever it had been. She coughed again, and wiped her face with the back of her hand, feeling the soggy silk glove that she'd forgotten she was wearing. And then it all came back to her: she'd pushed her hand through the force field into water. And then something had grabbed her – something powerful and muscled, something that had dragged her from the TARDIS like a parent pulling a child down a supermarket aisle.

Martha blinked, wondering again why it was so dark, wondering whether something had happened to her eyes. Wondering whether she was blind. She felt her heart begin to race in her chest as her panic began to grow. She heard a soft pattering noise above her. It sounded like rain on a tent.

And then she heard another sound: a tiny, tiny whispering noise. No – more like a scratching. No. That wasn't right, either. Where had she heard it before…?

Yes! That was it! It sounded like a cat, washing itself – with that strange scraping, slurpy noise they made. She sniffed cautiously. There was a dry smell, musky and animaly. Not unpleasant, but not particularly reassuring, either. And not cats.

Something touched the back of her outstretched hand and she gave a yelp, pulling it back and hugging it to herself. She heard the pattering of tiny feet and a gentle sniffing noise. More than anything, she felt embarrassed that she'd actually yelped.

Was she in some animal's burrow? Had she been snatched from the TARDIS by something and dragged to its nest? If she had, she could think of only one reason why a wild animal would do that. She suddenly remembered why the Doctor had brought her here, and her skin turned icy cold. He'd brought her here for breakfast.

Only *whose* breakfast...?

'We've got to tell Pallister!' said Col firmly.

'If I—' the Doctor said calmly, standing awkwardly near the door.

'Of course we tell Pallister,' replied Ty. 'Just not yet. It's the middle of the night!'

'So what?' countered Col. 'We wait until morning and then tell him that we've had a stranger in here – an offworlder – all night and that we didn't want to *wake* him?' He gave a snort.

'Perhaps I cou—' tried the Doctor again.

'He'll go mad, that's what he'll do.'

'And if we take him there now,' reasoned Ty, 'Pallister'll just have him locked up until morning anyway. And Candy says he has a friend out there.'

'He *says*,' Col scoffed. 'How do we know that—'

'Well,' the Doctor interjected, 'you could always try ask—'

'—he's telling the truth? Candy says he turned up out of nowhe—'

'Right!' bellowed the Doctor, instantly silencing the two

of them. 'Enough, as Donna Summer and Barbra Streisand once said, is *enough*!'

And Col and Ty shut up instantly and turned to him, their eyes wide with astonishment.

'If you'd have the good manners to argue *with* me, instead of *about* me, then maybe we could get this sorted,' he said. 'Do you lot take classes in interruption?' He threw a glance at Candy and raised a hand, his fingers spread out. 'One,' he counted off a finger, 'I was *not* stalking Candice.' He paused and frowned at the girl. 'Candy?' he puzzled. '*Candy?*' He shook his head sharply. 'Two…' Another finger was counted off. 'Yes, I *do* have a spaceship out there in the swamp, just like you do; and yes, my friend is – I hope – still inside it. And three.' He stopped and stared at his long, pale fingers. 'Three…' He sighed. 'I should have made the one about Martha into number three, shouldn't I? Two's just pathetic.'

Col, Ty and Candy were staring at him.

He stared back at them. 'What? *What?*'

'Who the future are you, "Doctor"?' demanded Ty. He could hear the quote marks in her voice. 'And where the future have you come from?'

The Doctor's shoulders sagged. Why was it *always* like this? With a resigned sigh, he reached into his inside pocket. Ty and Col – but not Candy, he noted – pulled back a little, as if he were reaching for a weapon.

'There!' he said triumphantly, brandishing the little wallet with the piece of psychic paper in it under their noses. 'That should answer your questions.'

He watched them smugly as they scanned it.

'You're a door-to-door carpet cleaner salesman?' said Col eventually.

'What?' snapped Ty, snatching the psychic paper from the Doctor's hand. 'This says he's Madame Romana, Astrologer to the Stars.' She looked at Col as if he'd gone mad, giving the Doctor the chance to grab the wallet back. He peered at it in dismay, shook it, peered at it again and gave a little moan.

'This,' he said firmly, brandishing it under their noses, 'is supposed to be waterproof. I knew I should have had it laminated…'

Candy wondered what she'd done, bringing this madman into the heart of their community. She'd introduced him to Professor Benson and Colin McConnon, thinking that they'd take to him in the same way that she'd done. And now here he was, talking gibberish about some bit of paper.

'I'm going to get Pallister,' said Col firmly, fixing the Doctor with a sharp look.

'Well maybe that's best,' said the Doctor defiantly. 'Then we can get this whole business sorted out, you can help me get my ship back from the swamp and I can be on my way. How's that sound?'

'Sounds fine to me,' Col said through gritted teeth.

There was a pause. No one moved, no one said anything.

'Go on then,' said the Doctor, waving Col away with the tips of his fingers. 'Run along to this Glenister, whoever he is. Tell him the Doctor will see him now.'

Col looked confused, glancing between Candy and Ty and the Doctor.

'That's right,' said the Doctor pleasantly. 'Leave me here.' He licked his lips hungrily. 'I haven't eaten in, ooh, hours and I'm feeling *very* peckish. What are you waiting for, Col? Go on – we'll be fine.'

'You're mad,' muttered Col. 'I'm not leaving you here with—' He broke off as the Doctor simply strode past him as if he'd forgotten he even existed. 'Oi!'

But the Doctor was suddenly ignoring him, examining the cages at the back of the lab. Ty's prides and joys, thought Candy. Her babies.

'Oooh!' cried the Doctor, staring into the cages. 'Otters! Otters with the faces of bears. Awwww…' he cooed suddenly. 'Aren't you *lovely*!'

'Doctor,' said Ty sharply, pushing past a speechless Col. 'I'd be careful, they have—'

'Rather large claws!' finished the Doctor sharply as one of the newer specimens reached through the bars and swiped at him. He pulled back just in time, fished out a pair of dark-framed, old-fashioned glasses and popped them on, 'And what *massive* teeth.'

One of the otters let out a little 'Squee!' at the sight of him.

He turned to the rest of them. 'All the better,' he grinned, 'to eat you with!'

'They're vegetarians, Doctor,' said Ty drily.

The Doctor turned back to the cages, and the otters and peered closer – but Candy noticed that this time he kept his hands firmly clasped behind his back.

'Ahh, yes… You can tell the incisors are for chewing

through wood. *Castoridae*, then.'

'Beavers!' said Ty in admiration. 'Although they're closer –
at least in appearance – to the *mustelidae*. Otters. They're not
quite mammals, though – closer to monotremes, really.'

'Egg-layers?' mused the Doctor. 'Interesting. And semi-
aquatic, judging by the webbing between the toes.'

He turned sharply and stared at Ty through narrow eyes
before taking off his glasses and slipping them back in his
jacket pocket.

'So why are they here? And why are they in cages?'

'Ty…' warned Col. He looked awkward, thought Candy,
torn between fetching Pallister and keeping watch over the
Doctor.

'We're studying them,' Ty said simply. 'Me and Col.'

'And why, considering all you've been through over the
past couple of months, would you be spending valuable time
studying these… these – have you got a name for them?'

'We just call them otters,' said Ty.

'Just "otters"? What's happened to human creativity,
imagination?' He shook his head, but Candy could see the
smile twinkling in his eyes. 'Love looking for the familiar
in the unfamiliar, you lot. Come on!' he spread his arms
wide. 'You're on a brand new world, brave new horizons,
boldly going where no one's ever gone before, blah, blah.
You should be making up exciting new names for things.'
He looked back at the cages. 'Call 'em "jubjubs",' he
suggested. 'Or "spingles". Always wanted to find something
called a spingle.' He paused. 'Or am I getting confused with
Spangles?'

'Let's just leave them as otters for the time being, shall we?' Col suggested a little icily.

'Fair enough,' agreed the Doctor brightly. 'Never one to interfere, me. So how come you have time to be studying otters? Shouldn't you be out building fences or digging wells or something rough and sweaty and butch?'

'I'm a xenozoologist, Doctor. I'm nearly 60 and, to be quite honest, there's not much else that I'm good at. Not unless the other settlers suddenly develop the need for an Earth Mother – or a Sunday Mother. And anyway, we're the advance guard, so to speak. We're here to set up the colony, investigate the local wildlife. Make sure it's all hunky dory for when the rest of the colonists arrive – if they bother coming now. Col,' she said firmly, turning away from the Doctor. 'Either go and get Pallister or sit down – just stop fannying around.'

Candy let out a little laugh. They were like an old married couple.

Col shook his head. 'Pallister'll go ape when he finds out—'

'When he finds out what?'

Everyone turned to the door. Standing there, in his grubby black suit, flanked by two other colonists – two *armed* colonists – was Pallister. Silently, they drew their guns and aimed them at the Doctor.

FOUR

There was complete silence. The Doctor stared from one gun to the other and then fixed Pallister with a firm gaze.

'I take it that you're Bannister.'

'Pallister,' corrected Pallister coldly.

'Bannister, Pallister…' said the Doctor airily.

'What are you doing on Sunday?' asked Pallister.

'Well,' said the Doctor, sucking in a breath. 'I thought I might wash the car, then have lunch down the pub – and maybe fall asleep watching the footie. Unless, of course, you're asking me on a date. In which case, I should point out that—'

'What are you doing on *our planet?*'

'Oh!' said the Doctor, wide-eyed. 'It's *your* planet is it? Sorry – I must have missed the sign on my way in.'

He suddenly turned his back on the three men in the doorway.

'Anyway,' he said blithely. 'What was I saying…? Oh yes.

These otters of yours…'

There were two heavy *clunks* from behind him as Pallister's men readied their guns. The Doctor took a deep breath and turned back to them.

'Good thinking, Rossiter. When faced with a puzzle, shoot it! When something comes along you don't understand, shoot it! When someone you've never met before says hello, shoot him! Nice policy.'

Candy swallowed nervously – the Doctor clearly didn't know Pallister. He might have been an officious nobody, but he was the officious nobody in charge of the Council, and he had a short fuse and a nasty temper when provoked. No one said anything.

'Right!' exclaimed Ty suddenly, pushing the Doctor aside and standing four-square in front of Pallister and his goons. 'This has gone on quite long enough!' She looked Pallister up and down as if he'd been caught smoking around the back of the schoolhouse. 'What is going on here, Pallister?' She glanced disdainfully at the two men, their guns raised. 'And put those down before someone gets hurt. You might be Chief Councillor, but since when was Sunday a military state? You can't just go stomping around with your little toy soldiers, waving guns at people. I mean,' she glanced back at the Doctor. 'Just look at him. Does he *look* like he needs an armed guard?'

Candy almost laughed at the expression on Pallister's face. He seemed totally thrown – not by the Doctor but by Ty.

'This is none of your concern, Professor Benson,' said

Pallister through gritted teeth.

'Oh, I think it is,' countered Ty, planting her hands on her ample hips. 'Remind me, *Councillor* Pallister,' she said, stressing his job title, 'but unless there's been a military coup overnight, Sunday's still a democracy, isn't it? And I'm pretty sure that the colony's constitution says that any *armed* action needs to be approved by the entire Council, not just one member.' She raised an eyebrow at the two guns. 'And I think waving guns around at a complete stranger in my lab probably comes under the heading of "armed action". Or has the constitution changed overnight too?'

'This man is a stranger,' replied Pallister, his words almost strangled in his throat. 'And as such he presents a potential threat.'

'Threat?' The Doctor's face lit up and he whirled around to face Ty and Col. 'Threat? Me?' He grinned. 'Well, I've been called a fair few things in my time – but the only people who've called me a threat are people who are up to no good.' He tipped his head back and looked down his nose at Pallister. 'Which would rather suggest that you, Mister Cannister, are up to no good, wouldn't it?'

Pallister opened his mouth to say something, but the Doctor just breezed on: 'Anyway,' he said simply. 'I think you need me. And I need you. I have a friend out there that I have to find, not to mention my spaceship. Wouldn't it make sense for us to work together, eh? A friend in need and all that? Helping hands…? Too many cooks…?'

Pallister just stared at him – and waved the two men forwards, as if instructing them to arrest him.

'This is mad,' said Ty as Pallister gave orders to one of the men to escort him to the detention centre. 'When the Council hears about—'

'When the Council hears about this,' Pallister finished her sentence, 'they'll back me up. We don't know where he's come from or what he's here for and, until we do, I have no intention of letting him run around the settlement.'

Ty clenched her fists, outraged at the man's audacity. 'They're not going to let you get away with this,' she warned him. 'You can't just go around pointing guns at people.'

'Desperate times call for desperate measures, Professor Benson.' He smiled crookedly. 'Believe me, you'll thank me when it turns out that this Doctor is here to cause trouble.'

Ty made a sharp tutting noise with her teeth and folded her arms over her bosom. 'But look at the state of him!'

As they argued, Candy noticed that the Doctor had pulled out the little black wallet that he'd shown to Ty and Col before, and was gently wafting it around behind his back.

'We only have his word for that,' Pallister thundered on. 'And, if you don't mind my saying, Professor, you seem very keen to believe his story. If he's just arrived in a spaceship – *if* – then how come we didn't see it land? No one's come forward to report anything, have they? We don't know how long he's been here. Maybe he's been sent from some other colony to interfere with us.'

'You're paranoid, Pallister! What if he's an adjudicator, sent from Earth for some reason? How's *that* going to look on your record, eh? Arresting and locking up an official from Earth – that's going to make you *very* popular, isn't it?'

And as if on cue, the Doctor's hand appeared between them, holding the black wallet he'd shown her earlier. She took it from him before Pallister could, and opened it again, expecting to find the card proclaiming the Doctor's status as 'Madame Romana'. Instead, she grinned at what she saw and thrust it out in front of Pallister.

'See!' she said, as he read it. Pallister's jaw dropped.

'Doctor,' he said smarmily, motioning instantly for his two assistants to lower their guns. 'Please, please accept my apologies.'

Ty could see that the Doctor was clearly trying to hold back a grin.

'Why didn't you say you were an adjudicator?' fawned Pallister.

'Well,' the Doctor replied, almost bashfully. 'We don't like to go about boasting about these things, you know.' He leaned close to Pallister and whispered in his ear. 'And we have to be *so* careful about the people we tell. I'm sure you understand.'

'Of course, of course. If you'd like to come this way,' Pallister said, his voice oily, 'I'll have an office sorted for you.'

He swept towards the doorway.

'How did you manage that?' whispered Ty as she and the Doctor followed.

The Doctor pulled a spooky face, wiggled his fingers and grinned wolfishly. 'Madame Romana,' he said in a strange accent. 'She know *everything*!'

* * *

Martha realised she'd fallen asleep again – although she had no idea how she'd managed it. The warmth of the burrow or the nest had dried her out a little, but she was still shivering. The rain and the rustling noises seemed to have stopped but, as she shifted about, lying on what seemed like dry leaves, they started up again.

She squinted and peered at the ceiling – was it getting lighter? She was sure she could see vague speckles of daylight, somewhere up above her. As she peered around her, trying to force her eyes to make something out, there was a flicker of movement, a dark shadow on a darker background.

'Hello?' she ventured, her voice croaky, her throat sore. 'Is there anyone there?'

There was no answer, but there was more movement.

'I'm not going to hurt you,' she added. *That's the way, girl,* she thought. *Keep your voice calm, steady.*

Down in front of her there was a thick, sploshing sound, like oily water being disturbed. The whispering and chittering around her stopped abruptly and all she could hear was the water. It was as though they were waiting for something.

Cautiously, she reached up and rubbed her face, feeling the dried mud and dirt caking her skin. As she moved, she heard tiny footsteps again, and squinted into the gloom. It was definitely getting lighter. Martha looked up at the ceiling, and realised that it was something like wickerwork: bits of grass and twigs plaited and threaded together, with the vaguest hint of rosy light showing through the gaps. How long had she been here?

'Doctor?' she ventured in a whisper. Perhaps he was here, unconscious, just a few feet away. 'Doctor!' she hissed again. There was no reply – just the squeaking from the distance, and the sound of the water.

As she stared into the gloom, she realised that she could see more than before. She was in a chamber, the woven ceiling forming a dome above her. It must have been about six metres across, with a darker, sunken area in the middle. Presumably that was where the water was. Something moved on the other side of the pit, and she could just about make out a slim, upright shape – a shape that immediately shrunk, like an animal dropping from its hind legs onto all fours.

And there were other things – paler things – only just visible in the waxing light. Martha narrowed her eyes and looked around: there was a lower level, just below hers, like a miniature Roman amphitheatre. Sprawled on it, across the pit from her, were three shapes. Could they be people? Perhaps others brought here in the same way she'd been brought. She peered into the darkness, willing her eyes to see…

… and then wished she hadn't. She felt the bile rising in her throat as she realised what she was looking at.

Laid out in the chamber, their hollow, sightless eyes staring straight back at her, were skeletons. Three of them. Three *human* skeletons. Their fleshless skulls gleamed pink as the light grew around her, their mouths open wide as if in a final, terrible scream.

* * *

Ty was amazed at the speed that things could move. One minute Pallister had been showing the Doctor into a barely furnished office – just a desk and a chair. And the next the Doctor was organising a mission to rescue his friend and his spaceship. It made her think even less of Pallister, if that was possible.

Pallister had spent a good ten minutes apologising until the Doctor had turned to him, fixed him with a steely glare, and told him, in no uncertain terms, to *go away* and leave him to it.

'That man,' said Ty as she peered out of the window into the pink dawn and watched Pallister scuttle away across the square to his house, 'is bad news. You know that, don't you?'

The Doctor smiled at her. 'I think I'd worked that one out.'

He bent over the desk on which a map – that Pallister had magicked up in seconds – had been unrolled, pinned down by an assortment of coffee cups and pots full of pencils.

'You're not an adjudicator at all, are you?'

The Doctor seemed shocked at her suggestion.

'Professor Benson!' he said, affronted. 'Are you accusing me of impersonating an officer of the Earth Empire?'

'We *have* an Earth Empire?'

He glanced at his watch. 'You will,' he smiled. 'Anyway…' He turned his attention back to the map, brushing away a few specks of mud that had fallen from his hair. 'We're *here* – and the TARDIS landed *here*.'

'That's your ship?'

'Spot on, Doctor Watson. Now, are there any beasties out there we need to be careful of? Candice told me about what happened. The flood. Sorry about that. But I'd hate to be responsible for the loss of any more of your people.'

'No,' she said after a moment's thought. 'Nothing that we know of – that's one of the reasons Sunday was approved for colonisation – fairly nice planet, all things considered. A bit wet and soggy, but warm. They were going to call it "Wetworld" – in contrast to "Earth" – before we vetoed it. Made us sound incontinent.'

'Very wise,' said the Doctor as he smiled, straightened up and took a deep breath.

'Can you round up half a dozen hefty bodies and some ropes? And if you've got any good swimmers around here, that'd help.'

'You're going to pull a spaceship out of the swamp with ropes and half a dozen bruisers?' Ty was incredulous. 'Just how big *is* this TARDIS of yours?'

Col started as Candy came back into the zoo lab.

'Jumpy,' she said with a tired smile.

'Thought you were with Pallister and his trained monkeys.' Col looked distant, thoughtful.

'Oh, I think the Doctor's got him firmly under his thumb,' Candy grinned, putting fresh coffee on to brew. She picked up her forgotten backpack from behind the door and pulled a face as she unzipped it: inside was a mess of smashed shell and gloopy egg.

'That's breakfast gone, then,' Col said gloomily.

'Give it an hour and the refec'll be open.'

'S'pose. So… this stuff about him being an adjudicator… Reckon it's true?'

Candy shrugged. 'Don't see why not.'

'I'm not sure anything's what it seems with the Doctor.'

'Why?'

Col said nothing, and there was a moment's awkward silence before he gestured towards the cages, where the otters were starting to wake up.

'Gonna give me a hand with this lot?' he said. Some of them were just stretching and yawning; others were pacing in tiny circles, patting down the leaves underneath them. One looked suspiciously like it was having a wee. And the one with the grey smudge on his ear, the one they'd had the longest, was fiddling with the padlock that held his cage shut.

'OK – what's what?'

Col checked the clipboard he'd been working on.

'Ty wants eight of them releasing – says they've reached maximum.'

'Smart and smarter again?'

Col nodded.

'Y'know,' said Candy thoughtfully, wandering over to the cage as the smell of coffee filled the lab, 'I wonder if it's *us*.'

'Us what?'

'Us that's making them smart.'

'You mean when we catch them they're dim and aggressive, and somehow contact with us ups their IQs? How would that work, then? They can't just be learning from us: we've made sure not to let them see us doing anything "clever".'

Candy wasn't sure, although it made as much sense as any of the other theories they'd come up with – and discounted: diurnal rhythms, food supply, separation from their families. Nothing seemed to really explain why the IQs of the otters seemed to rise the longer they were in captivity, before levelling out. Maybe they *were* picking it up from the humans. Candy knew she wasn't the brightest penny in the barrel, but she felt sure that the answer was staring them in the face.

Suddenly there was a knock at the door and, before Col could say anything, it slammed open and in staggered Orlo. Candy's friend was a stocky, beefy lad with a messy shock of black hair and a grumpy-looking face. He was carrying something large and square, draped with an old sack. It rattled and jumped in his arms, and he seemed only too pleased to put it down on the desk.

'You're a bit bright and early, aren't you?' asked Candy.

'Got woken up by all that fuss with the stranger,' Orlo explained. 'Thought I'd make an early start on getting Professor Benson another one. Feisty little beggar.' Candy pulled the sacking back – to reveal an otter in a cage, much like the ones at the back of the room, only smaller. It pulled back its black lips and hissed at them, incisors gleaming in the light.

'Something's got 'em spooked,' Orlo added.

'Maybe it's the Doctor,' Col ventured. 'A spaceship landing out there's bound to scare 'em a bit.'

He leaned in towards the cage – and a small, dark paw shot out through the wire mesh, razor-sharp claws extended, and slashed at him.

'Whoah!' he cried, jumping back. 'See what you mean, Orlo.'

'Something's wrong,' said Candy quietly, peering at the otter. It glared back at her viciously and let out a low, throaty growl. 'Something's *seriously* wrong.'

Martha tried not to look at the skeletons, but they drew her gaze to them. Even when she screwed her eyes shut so she couldn't see their grinning faces, they were still there. In her head. Screaming.

She felt sick and realised she was shivering. Not because it was cold, but because, no matter how much she tried, she couldn't help but think that these skeletons – these *people* – had been brought here like her. It wasn't like she hadn't had plenty of experience of skeletons and bodies and the mess and gore that the human body was capable of producing. After all, she was almost a doctor – and she'd seen enough death travelling with *the* Doctor. But she usually knew the histories of the people and bodies she'd examined, dissected. At the very least, she knew how they'd died. The fact that these had met their end on an alien planet, in an animal's nest, alone and probably terrified, made all the difference. Maybe this was a taste of her *own* future.

The growing light had revealed the chamber in more detail. At the other side was a small hole, through which a constant stream of otter-like things came and went, growling and grunting to themselves. They all looked the same, and Martha couldn't work out how many of them there might be. Occasionally, they would sit up on their back legs and watch her, their tiny eyes black as pitch. Sometimes, one or two of them would descend to the bottom level of the pit where black water slopped and swayed – as if there were something just under the surface, moving slowly. Usually, though, they just stared and growled.

She couldn't just sit here, she realised. Maybe that's what had happened to the others – they'd just sat there until they'd died, and then the otters had stripped the flesh from their bones.

Suddenly, the two by the edge of the pool jumped and scampered up onto the top level. They reared up on their back legs, squeaking and muttering.

Only then did Martha hear it: a deep sucking, slurping sound from below. Flecks of orangey-pink light, streaming through the canopy overhead, danced on the surface of the black water. And then it parted and slid aside as something reared up out of the pool.

Martha drew herself back against the wall of soil behind her. She cried out, instinctively, and saw the otters flinch.

It was as though the inky waters themselves were rising up. A tentacle, starting out thinner than her wrist and quickly growing to something wider than her waist, reared up in front of her. Water streamed and dripped from its glossy surface and it waved around in the air in front of her. Martha was reminded of a snail's eyestalk as it probed the air in the chamber, turning around, seeking, hunting.

Hunting *her*.

Slowly, it extended further, and Martha could see tiny granules streaming inside it as it came to rest just a foot from her face. And then, like a striking snake, it plunged towards her.

FIVE

It was icy cold, and Martha took a sharp breath in as the thing struck her face. But it was blocking her mouth and nose, squirming and writhing as though it were trying to enter her throat.

Desperately, she grabbed at it with her hands: it was shiny and hard like leather, yet viscous and flowing like oil, and her fingernails made no difference.

With slow and inexorable force, the tentacle pushed her back against the wall, flowing around her head. She could feel it creeping slowly over her ears as she struggled, smothered in its grasp. Dizziness washed over her as the oxygen in her lungs began to run out. In her panic, Martha kicked out at it. It felt like kicking a tree.

This is it, thought Martha through the fear, through the red haze clouding her mind. She dug her fingernails into the soil at her sides. *This is it.*

Her life didn't flash before her eyes. There were no visions of her family, no Mum, no Dad, no Leo or Tish. No Doctor.

There was just the redness and the cold and the pain in her chest.

And then, as she felt her body sag, there was a lightness, a feeling of letting go. Somewhere, way away in the distance, she could see a faint, blue light. Was that… was that where she was supposed to go? *Into the light?*

Then, suddenly, the light was gone, the coldness ripped from her and something pale burst out of the darkness.

'Martha Jones!' bellowed a voice that must have been her father's. 'Where are your Wellingtons?'

Martha took a huge, huge breath and the darkness swallowed her up again.

'Get her out,' ordered the Doctor, lifting the young woman's body up towards Ty and the others. They hesitated. 'Now!' he shouted, his face as dark as storm clouds.

Ty stepped back as three of the men who'd come with them to find the Doctor's ship rushed forwards and manoeuvred the unconscious girl – Martha – up and out of the otters' nest.

'What was *that*?' asked Ty as Martha was laid gently on the rain-soaked ground and the Doctor leapt nimbly out through the hole he'd made in the nest's canopy. The otters had scattered as the Doctor had crashed in.

'This?' The Doctor brandished a small, pen-like device in his hand – the device that had, somehow, made the… the *thing*… wrapped around Martha's head pull away and vanish into the water at the bottom of the nest.

'No – *that*,' Ty said, pointing back into the ruined nest.

The Doctor shook his head as he knelt down beside Martha and checked her pulse and breathing. 'Oh *that*? No idea. But at least we know it's not very partial to focused ultrasound, don't we?'

The Doctor pulled back Martha's eyelids to check her pupils. He seemed satisfied, and nodded.

'She'll be fine.' He paused and brushed at the hair on her temples. A pattern of tiny, red dots – pinpricks of blood – was visible. 'Not so sure about this, though,' he added, his voice low and concerned.

'Um, why's she dressed like that?' Ty asked, realising even as she said it that it probably wasn't quite the right thing to say under the circumstances. Martha was wearing an extremely dirty, extremely ripped silk ball-gown, and on her hands were elbow-length gloves. Ty couldn't imagine clothing more unsuited to Sunday. Was this how adjudicators dressed?

But the Doctor didn't answer, sitting back on his haunches and peering down through the hole in the roof of the nest.

They'd been tramping through the dawn-lit forest for almost half an hour, on their way to rescue the Doctor's ship – his TARDIS, as he'd called it – when suddenly he'd stopped.

'Hear that?' he said, holding up a hand for silence.

Ty hadn't heard anything.

'It's Martha!' he'd shouted, before haring off.

Ty and the others could only race after him. By the time they'd caught up with him, he was standing in the bottom of an otter nest, the roof caved in where he'd smashed through it. And he was holding out the pencil-thing with a glowing, blue tip – holding it against…

Ty didn't know *what* he'd been holding it against. All she could see in the gloom of the nest was something long and thick and dark, like a massive, glassy tentacle. Underneath it, as she peered closer, she could see arms… and legs… and then realised that it was a person.

And then suddenly the tentacle thing had pulled away and whipped back into the darkness with a mighty splash of water, drenching the Doctor and Martha.

'That thing,' he mused. 'I take it you've not seen it before?'

'Never,' Ty replied. 'And what was it doing in an otter nest?'

'Could it be some sort of symbiote? Something that lives with them, shares their nest? Maybe it's a pet. Maybe that's why you've never seen it?'

'Could be,' Ty considered. 'But I've seen inside a couple of nests before and never seen *anything* like that.'

'Well, we'll sort that out later – we've got to get Martha back to the settlement. If I were you, I'd take a look at the skeletons in there.'

'Skeletons?'

Ty glanced over into the ruined nest, and saw gleaming bones in the shadows on the other side of the pool.

'They might well be the people you lost in the flood,' the Doctor said.

She nodded, trying not to think about the implications of that statement. 'What about your ship?'

The Doctor threw her a dark look. 'I think that can wait, don't you?'

The hospital, the Doctor was relieved to see, was better equipped than he'd expected, considering the losses that the settlers had faced – a low, wide bungalow, partly constructed from prefabricated plastic panels, partly from wood, sitting at one edge of the square. The main ward was empty when the Doctor arrived. Martha was rushed to a bed and covered up with a blanket.

'This is Dr Hashmi – Sam Hashmi,' Ty introduced the Doctor to the short, elderly man who came over briskly as they arrived. 'Dr Hashmi – this is, erm, the Doctor.'

'And this is Martha,' said the Doctor swiftly. 'She's suffered hypoxia,' he said, and pulled aside the hair on Martha's temples. 'But the lack of oxygen's not what's worrying me – what d'you reckon this is?'

Sam peered closer at the speckle of red dots.

'Puncture wounds? Has she been attacked by something?'

'Oh yes!' said the Doctor sourly. 'A very big something. A very, *very* big something.'

'What?'

'Well if I knew that, I wouldn't be calling it "a very big something" would I?' he snapped and shook his head. 'Please, just do what you can for her, Dr Hashmi.'

Sam set about taking Martha's pulse and blood pressure before hooking her up to a body monitor whilst the Doctor stood back and watched, arms folded.

'She'll be fine,' Ty said, putting a hand on his shoulder. 'I'm sure of it.'

Suddenly, Candy came rushing in.

'Professor Benson!' she said. 'They said you'd gone out to…' Her voice tailed off as she saw Martha. She glanced at the Doctor and then back at Ty. 'Who's that?' she whispered.

'That,' the Doctor answered without turning, 'is Martha. My friend.'

'Oh,' said Candy. 'I'm sorry.'

'Someone's going to be,' muttered the Doctor. 'Or some*thing*.'

There was a long and awkward pause, and then the Doctor suddenly spun on his heel.

'Right!' he announced. 'Tell me all you know about these otters.'

Col had said they didn't need any more otters for a while, but Orlo found them fascinating enough to just watch. The weird thing was that they didn't seem to bear grudges. He'd caught and taken, what, over two dozen by now. And despite that – despite the way they struggled and scratched when he caught them – it didn't seem to make them more wary of him. He reckoned it was because he never hurt them and always let them go. In fact, crazy though it sounded, Orlo wondered if, somehow, the otters weren't actually *pleased* that he caught them. It made no sense, except that it was always the slower, more aggressive ones that he managed to catch (the cleverer ones just ran rings round him) – and when they were released, they were always smarter and more peaceable.

Let Professor Benson work that one out.

He squatted down at the top of a gentle rise, sheltering from the growing sun under a tree, and watched a couple of dozen of the otters diving in and out of the water, the light sparkling off their water and their silvery bodies. He could watch them all day.

Suddenly, all at once, the little fellers stopped their play. From where he was, he could hear squeaking and chittering, and saw that they were all looking at him. Some of them were standing upright in the shallows, others were along the bank, on all fours or up on their hind legs. And then – and this is when Orlo dropped his sandwich – they turned, as one, and looked back into the swamp. Automatically, Orlo followed their gaze. For a moment, he wondered what they'd heard or seen, but then something gleamed through the tops of the trees, something artificial.

Orlo raised his hand to shelter his eyes, squinted, and realised what he was seeing: it was a curved, mirror-like piece of metal, arcing over like a dolphin in mid-leap.

It was one of the fins of the *One Small Step*, the ship the colonists had arrived in. The ship that had been washed away in the flood. The ship that they never thought they'd see again.

And the otters were leading him to it.

'Orlo brought this one in this morning,' Candy said, pointing to the new otter.

It had been installed in one of the cages in the zoo lab and seemed to have calmed down a little. But it stared out at Ty, the Doctor and Candy suspiciously, with baleful little eyes. Col stood to one side, watching. Candy reckoned that he was still a bit wary of the Doctor: he kept looking him up and down, as if trying to work out what made him tick.

'He said it was a real handful,' Candy said.

'What are they like normally – when you catch them, that is?' The Doctor leaned forward and made squeaking noises at the otter. It glared back at him.

'Normally,' answered Ty, 'they're fairly docile. Sometimes they put up a bit of a struggle, but they calm down quite quickly.' She indicated one of the others, a plump little thing, with a greyish splodge on its right ear, happily curled up asleep. 'This one is our oldest resident. Brought him in last week. He was aggressive when we brought him in, but now he's a real sweetie – and *very* bright: he's got the maze down to under a minute.'

'The maze?'

She showed him a large side room, the floor laid out with a complex, wall-to-wall maze, half a metre high. The roof of it was a crazy-paving of mismatched plastic sheets to stop the otters just jumping over the walls to get to the food at the far end of the room. At various points along the route, there were levers and pulleys and sliding panels to operate to further test the otters' brainpower.

'We used it as a test of how bright they are. We don't really have the resources for anything else. Food goes at one end, an otter at the other, and we time how long it takes them to get to it. When we first brought him in, it took him almost an hour, and boy was he snappy about it.'

'That's not unusual, surely?' the Doctor frowned. 'Most intelligent creatures do that. It's called learning – start off bad, get better. Even humans are *quite* good at it.'

Ty pulled a face. 'I'm a zoologist, Doctor – I've worked with animals for years, and with people before that. And there's something just *wrong* about this: it's the speed with which their learning curve increases – and then suddenly plateaus out after about two days. If the otters were capable of learning so quickly, it'd be them building a city here, not us.'

'Oh, don't judge alien species by your own,' the Doctor said, making a sucking noise. 'There are as many types of intelligence and learning as there are worlds out there.' He took the clipboard from her and scanned it, and again Candy saw the sharpness in his eyes. 'Still, I see what you mean. The otters have clearly evolved to fill an environmental niche, and their speed of learning is a bit at odds with it, I'll grant you.'

Candy cut in. 'I wondered if it was us.'

'*Us?*' Ty was puzzled.

'You think proximity to humans is making them smarter?' said the Doctor. '"Brains by osmosis." As ideas go, it's not a bad one, but you'd think that they'd carry *on* getting smarter, wouldn't you? Oh hello – what's this, then?'

Candy peered around Ty as the Doctor moved closer to the new arrival's cage. He pulled something out of his pocket and she saw that it was the torch he'd had out in the forest. He aimed it at the wall behind the cages and turned it on. A spot of bright blue light appeared on the wood. The otter gave a threatening little *grrrrr* at the Doctor's device and burrowed into the leaves in the cage.

'What are you looking at?' asked Ty, trying to see. 'Oh.'

She stopped. Because highlighted by the Doctor's torch, scratched into the wall, was a shape: a rectangle, about twice as tall as it was wide, with a little bump on the top.

'What is it?' whispered Candy. 'Did the otter do it?'

'It's the right width for one of their claws,' said the Doctor, tracing the outline of it with the beam from his device.

'But what *is* it?' repeated Ty.

'That,' said the Doctor, a very worried edge to his voice, 'is my spaceship. That's the TARDIS.'

'Looks like it's our lucky day, then,' came an out-of-breath voice from the door. They both turned to see Orlo, sweating and panting and supporting himself on the doorframe. 'Because now we've got *two* ships! I've found the *One Small Step*!'

Martha moaned and opened her eyes. She was lying in some sort of hospital ward – a pretty basic one, she had to admit, but a hospital ward nonetheless. Most of it seemed to be made out of wood. Basically, a big log cabin.

A wide window on the other side of the room gave out onto a view of low, spaced-out houses, built of a mishmash of wood and bits of plastic and metal. It looked like a low-tech Butlins. The light outside was very strange, though. Dull orange, like some sort of weird twilight. Martha wondered how long she'd been here, and whether she'd slept through a whole day. Of course, she realised, that meant nothing. A day on another planet could be any length, couldn't it? And the night she'd spent in the chamber had seemed pretty short. As the memory came back to her, she suddenly felt her face grow cold and clammy. The hairs on her arms stood up as though an icy shadow had passed over her.

Where was the Doctor? She had a vague memory of him peering into her face, but she wasn't sure whether she'd imagined it. She looked up suddenly as a wave of darkness flitted across the window – but there was nothing there. Martha shook her head. She was *sure* she'd seen something, something huge and shadowy. Maybe they'd given her some painkillers or sedatives that were making her mind play tricks.

And then out of the corner of her eye, she saw something sinuous flick out from under the bed, whipping across the floor before it pulled back out of sight. Martha flinched, gritted her teeth and pulled her hands up to her chest. Her mouth was dry. Slowly, she leaned out over the side of the bed and peered down, half-afraid of what she might see. Visions of huge, slimy tentacles crowded at the back of her mind, thrashing about like hungry tongues, threatening to squeeze her sanity out.

But the polished wooden floor was clear. She tried to swallow but her mouth was like cotton wool.

On the cabinet beside her was a glass of water. She picked it up gingerly, her hand shaking, and swallowed it down in one gulp. Instantly she felt a lot better. The coolness, the *wetness* of it felt so good, so right. For a moment, she just wanted to dive into an icy pool, or a river or the sea…

She shook her head, suddenly disorientated, and the warm, hard surroundings of the hospital room swam back into view. Looking around for more water, she noticed a clipboard and a pen on the cabinet. Setting down the glass, she picked them up and saw they were her notes. Even though she hadn't quite finished medical training, she knew more than enough to be able to tell that she was in pretty good condition. Heart rate, blood pressure, blood oxygen – all normal enough. That was a relief. There was mention of some drug that she'd never heard of. Maybe it was a tranquilliser. Didn't seem likely they'd give her anything that could cause hallucinations, surely. Stress, Martha decided firmly. That's what it was. She'd been through a lot – dragged from the TARDIS, thrown into a pit with a load of animals and an underwater monster and then nearly killed by it. Anyone would have hallucinations after that.

She just needed to rest, that was all. Absently, she unclipped the pen and tapped it against the clipboard as she lay back on the bed…

A couple of kilometres down-river, at the point where the tidal wave had deposited its makeshift dam, the banks on both sides were a seething mass of otters: hundreds and hundreds of them, running hither and thither, like a colony of ants. They were diving into the water and returning with paws full of mud, depositing it on the banks, slapping it into numerous rapidly growing hillocks.

Like creatures obsessed, they were steadily breaking down the dam that had held the settlement in its watery grave for all these months.

SIX

'And there's more,' gasped Orlo, bending over and resting his palms on his thighs as he struggled for breath.

'What?' demanded Col, suddenly concerned. Orlo shook his head, unable to get the words out.

'The… the settlement,' he finally managed. 'The first settlement.'

'What about it?'

'You can see it. Just the tops of the buildings. But they weren't there yesterday, I'd swear. I saw them when I went to check on the ship.'

'The water level must be falling,' mused the Doctor, tapping his bottom lip with his fingers.

'We need to tell everyone,' Candy said. 'Get them all out there—'

'Hold your horses a second,' the Doctor cut in. 'If the water level's suddenly falling, it has to be for a reason. The last thing you want is everyone out there, scampering around like excited schoolkids on a fieldtrip when we don't really know what's going on.'

'Doctor,' Ty said, 'this is *our* colony. And this is the biggest thing to happen since the flood. If we can get the settlement and the ship back…' She let the sentence tail off, leaving the possibilities unspoken.

'You'll what? Fly back home?'

Ty was aghast.

'No way! We're here for the duration, Doctor. But if the ship's accessible, it means we'll be able to set up another generator, using the ship's power core. We can stop having to burn wood every time the generator we've got packs in. And if we can find the smart-fabricator, we can get to work on the settlement properly.'

The Doctor's eyes narrowed suddenly.

'Power core…? Just what kind of ship is this *One Small Step* of yours? What model?'

'It's a *mark II world-builder*,' said Candy.

The Doctor's expression froze, his brows set in a thundery line.

'A *mark II*? You're sure? Not the *mark III*?'

Candy shook her head.

'Deffo – me and Orlo used to use the shipbrain on the journey for learning stuff. The welcome screen definitely had "*mark II*" on it. Why? What's wrong?'

The Doctor had slumped back against the desk, his arms folded.

'You've got a problem with that?' asked Ty. Candy could see she was getting ratty.

'Not me that's going to have the problem with it,' he

said darkly. 'I mean, you lot leave the Earth because it's overpopulated and polluted, looking for something new and better – and what do you do? You bring a *mark II world-builder* with you. A ship powered by one of the most filthy fission reactors your species has ever come up with?' He shook his head. 'It's like moving out of your house because the roof's leaking, and before you've even unpacked, you're up a ladder, ripping the slates off the new one!'

'And you'd know all about setting up a colony, would you Doctor?' Ty's voice was edged with defensiveness.

'Well I know quite a bit about how you humans go about it.' There was something about how he said 'you humans' that made the hairs on Candy's arms prickle. 'I've lost count of the number of times that I've sung your praises, you know, told everyone about how endlessly inventive, how incredibly adventurous you lot are. Snatching victory from the jaws of defeat, battling against the odds, yadda yadda yadda.' He fixed Ty with a dark gaze. 'I tend to forget about the times when you're stupid, stubborn and fail to learn from your mistakes.'

Ty was gritting her teeth, hands on hips.

'Setting up a new colony costs money, Doctor. Have you any idea how much a fusion generator costs? We bought the *One Small Step* because it had a fission generator and a spare core. It's the spare that we're using to generate our electricity. We were lucky that we didn't lose it in the flood, otherwise we'd be struggling by on wood-burning and nothing else. When Sunday's established and the rest of the colonists arrive then we'll trade the fission core in for a fusion unit.'

'And until then, you'll go on risking polluting this new Eden of yours, will you? Digging up uranium, creating waste that will still be around for your great-great-great-grandchildren to cope with. What's wrong with solar? Planetothermal? Wind-power? Tidal power, for goodness' sake!'

'Not viable here – believe me, we looked into them. And the experimental tidal generators we set up were washed away in the flood. Don't judge someone 'til you've walked in their shoes, Doctor,' Ty warned.

'And what about the ship?' the Doctor added after a pause. 'What about the generator aboard that? Just abandoned out there in the swamp, up to its gills in water.'

'These things are built for safety, you know. It's not as if all the uranium is just going to wash out into the water.'

He just shook his head, sadly.

'Anyway,' he said with a sigh, 'first things first. We need to take a look at the settlement, see if we can work out why it's suddenly become visible. And *then* we can take a look at your ship, make sure you're not doing to Sunday what you've already done to the Earth. If the power core of the *One Small Step* has been breached, I'd dread to think what it might be leaking into the water. Orlo – you up for taking us out there?'

Orlo rolled his eyes, but nodded.

'Finish your coffee,' the Doctor said, patting the lad on the shoulder. 'I want to check on Martha first. Back in a mo.' He glanced around the room as he left. 'Where's Col, by the way?'

Candy looked around: the Doctor was right – without so much as a 'See you', Col had gone.

Martha was asleep, her eyes flickering and darting under her eyelids.

'She's having some very vivid dreams,' the Doctor muttered, making Dr Hashmi jump. 'How is she?'

Sam indicated the medical monitor, suspended above Martha's bed.

'She looks fine,' he said. 'Nothing that a few hours' sleep won't cure.'

'And what about those marks?' The Doctor indicated the pattern of dots on Martha's temples, now faded to little more than a mild rash. 'Make anything of them?'

'Probably where that thing grabbed her. Hopefully nothing more than a graze.'

'Hmm,' said the Doctor. 'D'you have the results of her bloodwork? I'd like to be sure she's not been infected with anything. Anything *alien*.'

'I've given her some shots, although the pathogens around here are fairly benign. I wouldn't worry that she's picked anything too bad up.'

The Doctor fixed him with a stare.

'I'd like to be sure,' he said.

Sam checked his watch.

'Well they should be back in an hour or so – sorry it's taken so long, but our path lab is a bit makeshift. Doubles up for just about every bit of bioanalysis we need around here. And apparently they've brought back some skeletons

– from the nests. Found quite a few of them. They're having a look at them to see if they can work out who they are, and how they died.'

The Doctor nodded silently, took Martha's hand and gave it a squeeze.

'Take good care of her,' he said.

He leaned in over Martha.

'And you take good care of yourself, Martha Jones. We've got a date, remember? At *Tiffany's*.' He gave a little chuckle. 'But before that, we'll need to get you a new frock. Yellow, I think – that's the colour of nobility on Arkon. Should suit you down to the ground. Or the knees, at least.'

And with that, he was gone.

Plucking a pen from the breast pocket of his coat, Sam picked up the clipboard from beside Martha's bed, noticing that someone had doodled all over it. It took him a few moments to realise what the circular sketch was: a picture of a planet, with rough continents drawn in. And engulfing it, with eight smooth fingers or talons, was a hand.

Pallister scratched at the stubble on his pointed chin and wondered for the third time that morning whether he shouldn't take an hour off to go home and have a shave and a shower. It didn't do for the Chief Councillor to look so scruffy, not when there was an adjudicator around. He chewed his lip, thoughtfully. Maybe looking a bit worn and frazzled had its advantages, though – it would look like he cared more about his duty than his appearance.

Besides, he couldn't really spare the time. The arrival

of this Doctor was a pain in more ways than one. Pallister peered out of his office window as he saw the Doctor cross from the hospital back to the zoo lab. A few of the settlers out in the square watched him go and began talking amongst themselves. Word was spreading already: Earth had sent an adjudicator! The Chinese whispers had started. His assistant, Eton, had come tapping at his door not ten minutes ago, claiming people were saying a recovery mission was on its way to Sunday, and that they were all to be evacuated.

'Rubbish!' Pallister snapped. 'Go back out there and stop these stupid rumours before we have everyone out in the square with their suitcases packed.'

'Pardon me for asking, sir – what's he here for?'

'That's something between him and me – and the Council,' Pallister added quickly. 'There's a meeting this evening and you'll all be told in the fullness of time.' Eton just stared at him. 'At the appropriate juncture,' Pallister added more firmly.

'Yes, sir. Very good, sir.'

'Now go and stop those rumours, Eton – and if I hear any more of them, I'll know who to blame, won't I?'

Eton could only stammer an apology as he ducked out of the room.

As the door closed, a sudden sense of cold dread swept through Pallister. What if the Doctor were here to investigate *him*? No, that was impossible. There was nothing to investigate, was there? His election had been… well, it had *seemed* open and above-board. He'd kept the promises he'd made to the key families that had voted him in: better houses, higher priority on work rotas, that sort of thing. It was hardly an adjudication matter, surely. Everything he was doing here was for the good of the colony – no adjudicator could argue with that. Solid leadership. A single hand taking charge.

So why was the Doctor spending so much time with Benson? Why wasn't he in the office that Pallister had so kindly provided for him?

Too many questions, he thought, picking up a pencil and bending it in his fingers. Too many questions and so far not a single answer.

He swore as the pencil snapped – and there was another knock at the door.

Ty had packed a thermos of coffee and some sandwiches for their hike to the original Sunday City. Orlo looked a bit reluctant to trudge back there – especially after racing back to the zoo lab at full tilt. But with a bit of chivvying from the Doctor, he soon went along with it.

'Should have brought Candy,' Orlo said as they made their way through the forest. 'She's a good swimmer – she could have gone down there and taken a look.'

'The last thing we want,' said the Doctor – who'd taken off his jacket and slung it over his shoulder, 'is anyone diving into those waters.'

'You think there might be more of those things that attacked Martha?' asked Ty, struggling to keep up with the Doctor's pace. The reports that had returned along with the recovered skeletons suggested that quite a few of the nests might have had creatures living in their water pools. Eleven skeletons had been found, all in the same state, in five different nests. And in four of those there had been signs of *something* thrashing about in the water.

'I wouldn't be surprised,' he answered. He seemed distracted – no doubt worried about his friend. Ty watched him carefully, trying to work him and Martha out. Were they a couple? Just friends? Work colleagues? If they were a couple, Ty thought wryly, then Martha was one lucky woman.

She was pleased that their earlier spat seemed to have been forgotten. She was sure that the Doctor's heart was in the right place, but, really, he couldn't begin to understand the difficulties and costs involved in setting up Sunday. They'd had no choice but to go for the *mark II world-builder* ship – it wasn't like they had an unlimited budget. But still, she knew where he was coming from on this. She just didn't like to think about it too much.

'So why haven't we seen anything of these tentacled things before?' she asked, getting back on track,

The Doctor could only shrug.

'Maybe they've been hiding. Maybe they only live in the otter nests. Maybe the meteorite disturbed them…' His voice tailed off. 'Now there's a thought…'

'What?' asked Ty. 'That the meteorite disturbed them?'

The Doctor didn't answer but strode out ahead. Ty sighed exasperatedly. Fascinating and charismatic the Doctor might be; but he could also be *very* irritating.

* * *

The late-morning air was pleasantly warm and filled with the scents of an alien world. The Doctor breathed deeply, savouring every breath. The rain had washed the air clean, left it citrusy, piney. They said that travel broadened the mind – they never mentioned how it broadened the senses too. Maybe if he hadn't been so worried about Martha and the TARDIS he'd have used one of his own senses – his *common* sense – and put two and two together. Sometimes, he thought, he could just be *too* clever.

Ty had said she'd never seen the tentacled things that had attacked Martha before. Yet she was a zoologist and she'd spent a good few months studying the animal life in this area of Sunday. How likely was it that she could have missed them – or at least missed clues to their existence? So if the creatures hadn't been around before the flood, and now they were…

Two and two, he thought worriedly. *Two and two…*

The three travellers reached the peak of a small hill overlooking the lake where the first Sunday City had drowned that night. Strange how the site of such a tragedy could look so peaceful – almost idyllic. He could almost imagine rowing boats drifting gently across it. He remembered the map that Ty had shown him: like Earth, Sunday was mainly ocean. Unlike Earth, however, it was almost *entirely* ocean, with a speckle of islands, large and small, girdling its equator. He imagined that the planet had been chosen as a good colony world precisely because of all that water. And, ironically, it had been that very water that had nearly wiped the colony out. But humanity would prevail. It usually did. They were tough old sticks. Even if they *had* hoiked a great big old mucky nuclear power plant light years across space.

Orlo had been right – sticking up out of the placid water, like the prows of capsized ships, were the tops of at least a dozen buildings. Now they were grey and green, matted with silt and algae. Even the night's rain hadn't washed them clean. The Doctor tried to imagine them, shining and new, as they must have been before the meteorite struck.

He scanned the forest for any sign of the *One Small Step* – but it was a couple of kilometres out of sight beyond the trees.

'The water's dropped even further,' said Orlo in disbelief, discarding his backpack by the side of the otter cage that he'd abandoned earlier. 'At this rate it'll be dry in a couple of days!'

The Doctor shielded his eyes from the rays of the orange sun, now almost directly overhead, and gazed out along the river. It curved around a chunk of green headland and disappeared towards the sea.

Ty was at his side, and he could have sworn she'd read his mind.

'Take us at least an hour,' she said. 'To walk out to where the river silted up. That's what you're thinking, isn't it?'

'If the water level's dropping this quickly,' the Doctor said, lowering his hand from his eyes, 'then it must be going somewhere. And short of someone pulling a plug out of the bottom of the river, the only sensible place is back to the sea.' He looked her in the eye. 'Yes. That's what I'm thinking about. Up for it?'

Candy was puzzled – not to mention worried – about Col. He'd disappeared.

She searched all over, asking everyone she met. At first, she assumed he'd just wandered off somewhere. But that wasn't like Col. He rarely went out into the forest or the swamps on his own, and then only when he really had to. His duties were all at the settlement, in the offices, zoo lab or in the kitchens.

It was the in the refectory that Candy finally found a clue. Janis, the duty cook, told her that she'd seen Col not twenty minutes ago. He'd said something about the *One Small Step* – with an oddly worried look on his face. And then he'd snatched a couple of wrapped duck sandwiches from the counter and rushed off.

It wasn't much to go on, thought Candy, but it was all she had. So she grabbed a waterproof jacket from a hook near the door and set off into the forest.

It didn't take her long to pick up his trail. Candy had plenty of experience of tracking animals, and she was quick to spot the signs of Col's passage: a broken branch here, a footprint there. The fact that Col wasn't a small man made the footprints deeper and easier to spot. But she was relieved when she came across one of the sandwich wrappers, flapping on a branch – now she *knew* that she was on the right track. The route to the ship followed the path to the old settlement for a couple of kilometres and then veered right, inland. The flood had washed it a lot farther than anyone had expected, according to Orlo, and the journey took her through relatively unfamiliar territory. The forest thinned out closer to the water, replaced by lower bushes and soggier ground. Fortunately, for once, there was no sign of rain. Before she knew it, she was breaking out of the vegetation at the peak of a small hill; and standing not a hundred yards away, slumped over on its side in a half-drained river, was the *One Small Step*. It was a sorry sight.

She, along with the other settlers, had seen it in all its grandeur before take-off back on Earth. Launched from just outside Mbandaka in the Democratic Republic of Congo (because of its proximity to the Equator and the ease of launching), the ship had blazed golden in the evening sun, eliciting gasps of delight from all of them. Back then it had shone like a star.

But much of that glory had been burned away by the launch and planetfall. And by the time the settlers had set foot on their new home, it was looking much the worse for wear. All those months under water had done nothing to improve matters. Only the three fins (totally functionless, Orlo had told her, there simply to look good!) retained any of their shine. One of them rose to the roof of the forest, albeit at something of a lopsided angle.

The flood had painted the rest of the ship in shades of mud-brown, slime-green and disaster-grey. And then the rain had streaked rivulets of cleanness down its side. Candy slithered down the bank towards the river, spotting Col's footprints in the gloopy mud as she went. She thought about shouting Col's name, but something made her hold back. She felt a bit guilty, but she wanted to find out what he was up to, and giving him advance warning that she was on her way might not be a good idea. As she reached the ship, she saw that the passenger ladder was still intact. Bent at a weird angle, but, amazingly, still intact. It dangled a couple of feet from the mud – from where Col's footprints ended.

Candy looked up across the vast, barrelling curve of the ship, and noticed a dozen holes in the plating, a shattered window on the flight deck and a vast gouge along the ship's flank… She sighed. It would take a lot of work to make this fly again. Gritting her teeth, Candy reached for the ladder, grabbed firmly, and began to haul herself up.

Whilst Martha slept, she dreamed. A dream more vivid, more solid than any she'd had before.

She was standing in a lake – a vast, mirror-smooth lake – that stretched to the horizon all around her. The sky above was a deep blue, untouched by clouds. High overhead burned a tiny, white sun, but when she stared up at it, it didn't hurt her eyes. The lake must have been shallow, since it only came up to her knees.

Suddenly, as she looked down, the waters around her began to froth and seethe as something under the surface moved violently. She stared at the boiling white foam rising rapidly around her, unable to move, unable to cry out. Something strong and powerful grabbed her ankles and began to pull her under. Thrashing her arms about, trying to remain upright, Martha opened her mouth to scream as the water flooded in—

—and then she was sitting bolt upright in the bed, sobbing and shuddering.

'Doctor!' she heard a voice call out – a girl's voice, close to hand.

Martha opened her eyes to see a young woman, probably in her late twenties, standing at the side of the bed. She was wearing dark-blue combat trousers with lots of pockets and a light-blue shirt. Her head was shaved, and an intricate ivy-leaf tattoo crept up the right-hand side of her neck and coiled around her ear.

She'd said 'Doctor!' Martha suddenly realised, and looked round, hoping to see…

But the man who came rushing over wasn't the Doctor at all. Wasn't *her* Doctor. He had a pale green coat on – at least Martha imagined that it was pale green: the orange light flooding in from the window made judging colours a bit tricky – with a name badge that read 'Dr Sam Hashmi'.

'It's OK, it's OK,' Martha said as Dr Hashmi tried to make her lie back down. 'Just a dream. I'm fine.'

But this doctor clearly didn't think she was, and began checking her pupils.

'I'm fine,' Martha insisted after a few seconds. 'Honestly. I could do with a drink of water, though.'

The doctor nodded and passed her the glass from beside the bed that she'd drunk from earlier, now refilled. She gulped it down gratefully, feeling it soothe the burning she felt inside.

'You're Martha, aren't you?' asked the girl. 'I'm Carolina, the duty nurse – the Doctor rescued you from the otters.'

'The what?'

'He and Ty – Professor Benson – found you in one of the otter nests.'

Otter nests? What was she talking about? Martha screwed up her eyes and tried to remember. And suddenly it all came back to her again: the chamber, the animals in there. And…

'Something tried to kill me,' she said steadily, trying not to let herself get worked up again. 'Something—'

'We know,' interrupted Sam, refilling her water glass and passing it back to her. She glugged it down, not caring that it spilled down her chin and onto the hospital gown they'd dressed her in while she'd slept. 'The Doctor told us. How are you feeling?'

Martha just shook her head.

'Lousy,' she said – and managed a laugh. 'We were supposed to be going for a swanky breakfast… Should've known it'd go wrong somehow. Where is he?'

'The Doctor?' said Sam. 'I think he's gone with Ty – back to the settlement. The first one.'

Martha's confusion clearly showed on her face.

'The one that drowned in the flood.' Carolina looked puzzled that Martha still wasn't getting it. 'Sunday City.' After a second or two, she glanced at Sam, worried.

'I think you need to rest,' he said, obviously sharing Carolina's concern. 'A few more hours' sleep and you'll be fine.'

'Sunday? Where's Sunday? We were supposed to be going to New York.'

'New York?' said Carolina. 'Well, you're about a hundred light years off-course for New York, babes.'

Martha let her head flop back on the pillow with a sigh.

'He's done it again, hasn't he?'

'Who?' asked Carolina. 'Done what?'

'The Doctor – he's gone and got us lost again.' She shook her head, smiling.

'But I thought he was an adjudicator – sent here from Earth.'

'A what?' Martha struggled to sit up again. There was something about the word that sounded very official, very serious.

'An adjudicator,' repeated Carolina. 'That's what he told Pallister – Chief Councillor Pallister.'

'Ohhh,' said Martha after a couple of seconds, realising that – as usual – events were starting to run out of control. 'Right. Yeah. That's right – he's an adjudicator.' She watched Carolina and Sam's expressions to check she was getting it right. 'From Earth. It's just that…' Martha struggled for a moment. As if it wasn't bad enough that she'd woken up in a hospital straight out of *Little House on the Prairie*, she now had to keep up with whatever hare-brained explanation the Doctor had given these people. 'It's just that we were supposed to stop off in New York for breakfast first. *Before* coming here.' She rolled her eyes theatrically. 'Typical, eh? He decided to come straight here and didn't think to tell me. Isn't that *so* like him!'

Carolina glanced at Sam. Martha couldn't quite work out whether they'd sussed what she was up to or whether they just thought she'd gone mental. Oh well, the Doctor could sort it all out when he got back. All she had to do was to play the dopey patient for a while. For a trainee doctor, how hard could that be?

'We'll let you rest,' Sam said after a few seconds, checking the monitor hanging above her head. 'By the way…' He pulled a piece of paper out of his pocket, unfolded it, and handed it to her. 'Does this mean anything?'

Martha stared at the paper. It was the sheet that had been on the clipboard earlier, the one with her medical notes. But now, scrawled all over it, was a picture. For a moment it made no sense; but then her mind clicked into place – and it all came flooding back…

Martha lashed out at Carolina and the doctor with her fists. She screamed a deep, animalistic howl, kicking off the sheets and staggering to her feet. The two of them backed away, terrified at the change that had come over the girl. Her eyes blazing, spittle flying from her lips, Martha raised her hands like claws, and advanced towards them.

SEVEN

'Well, well, well… what have we here…?' The Doctor, Ty and Orlo crawled over the peak of the hill and peered down the slope to where the river narrowed. Swarming around the site of the dam that was blocking the flood's retreat, splashing in and out of the water, were hundreds and hundreds of otters. Ty wondered whether the Doctor's desire for a *new* otter was just crazy talk, or whether there was some sort of method in his madness.

'It's incredible,' whispered Ty. In all her months of studying the otters, she'd never seen so many of them in one place. 'I had no idea they were so social.' She shook her head, realising that she'd have to ditch half the notes she'd made for her grand textbook on the creatures.

'Organised, yes,' muttered the Doctor. 'Not so sure about social, though.'

'But *look!*'

'I know, I know – but don't you think there's something a bit odd about it. A bit manic. A bit *forced*.'

Ty looked again. She could see what he meant. The frenzy with which the otters were diving in and out of the water, carrying little pats of mud in their paws and slapping them onto the dozens of dark grey piles along the banks, was almost comical.

'You don't think this is natural?'

'Spot on. There's something very *un*natural about this whole thing.' He rolled onto his side and faced Orlo.

'So you're up for catching us another of those little fellers?'

Orlo grinned.

'Good lad. Come on!'

Ty huffed herself to her knees and watched as the Doctor, equipped only with his jacket, and Orlo, carrying a sack, set off cautiously down the slope. She watched as the Doctor and Orlo split up and started a pincer movement on one of the mud piles. From where she squatted, she could see everything, and it was clear that the two men were trying to keep the pile between them and the otters. The Doctor nodded to Orlo as yet another otter splashed up onto the bank and, bouncing along on its hind legs, headed towards the pile with a great big glob of mud in its paws. A steady but growing trickle of water spilled over the top of the dam, back towards the sea.

Orlo might have been a big lad, Ty thought, but he couldn't half move fast when he had to. Holding the sack out in front of him, he headed down the slope, slipping behind the otter to cut it off from the rest. A couple of the others threw him a glance, and Ty half-expected them to raise the alarm. But surprisingly, they finished slopping their mud onto the ground, dropped to all fours, and simply scampered back down to the water, vanishing into it with brief, silver flashes.

Now Orlo was in position between the otter and the river. The little creature paused and turned. When it saw Orlo, it cocked its head on one side, clearly unsure what to do.

The Doctor crept out from behind the mud pile, his coat held out in front of him. He must have made a noise, because the otter suddenly turned its head. Ty could almost see the puzzlement – and then the panic – in its eyes. With a sudden amazing turn of speed, it darted to one side of Orlo. But Orlo was quick. He sidestepped and lunged for the creature. The otter was confused and stopped sharply before backing up, casting nervous looks over its shoulder at the advancing Doctor. Ty felt her heart pounding: she never thought that she'd be quite so excited at the sight of two grown men trying to catch a small animal. A twinge of guilt struck her. All her life she'd been a champion of animal rights, and the decision to go into zoology had been part of that – an attempt to understand the animal world, and to bring that understanding to a wider public. The idea of getting even a tiny bit excited over two men chasing a small (if not quite defenceless) alien otter with only a jacket and a sack would once upon a time have appalled her. Was she just getting old, or was she becoming more pragmatic?

The Doctor feinted left and, as the otter slipped to the right, he threw himself towards it, arms and jacket outstretched – and missed by a mile. The otter – clearly deciding that he'd be better off racing uphill and around the two sweating humans – bounded away, galloping as fast as its little paws would carry it.

Orlo staggered after it, sack raised, as the Doctor rolled along the ground, recovered spectacularly, and sprang to his feet. His eyes wide and crazy, he chased up the hill, hot on the heels of the otter.

'This is madness!' cried Ty with an exasperated sigh and stood up, in plain view of the little creature. It scrabbled to a halt, its paws digging into the soft mud and coarse grass. With a shake of her head, Ty reached into her pocket, pulled out a tranq-gun, and shot the otter in the shoulder.

Two seconds later, it gave a little wheeze and toppled over.

The Doctor heaved himself to his feet, looking even more mud-spattered than he had done the previous night, and fixed Ty with a stunned glare.

'You had that in your pocket all along?' he growled. 'That.' He jabbed a finger at the tranq-gun, still in her hand. '*That!*'

'Well you didn't think I'd come out here unarmed after everything that's happened, did you?'

'And you didn't think to use it *earlier*?' He shook droplets of mud from his jacket – and Ty suspected that they weren't landing on her totally by accident. 'Have you any idea how hard it is to find a good dry-cleaner in this part of the galaxy?' He held the jacket out at arm's length and stared at it sadly. 'Ruined,' he announced. '*Ruined!*'

'Oh come on!' laughed Ty, pocketing the gun. 'Don't tell me you didn't enjoy that?'

The Doctor narrowed his eyes at her, but said nothing. Orlo came panting up, the tranquillised otter cradled in his arms. Asleep, Ty thought, it looked as sweet and friendly as they always did – possibly because its mouth was shut and its claws were sheathed.

'Let's get this into the cage and back to the lab,' the Doctor said, with sudden briskness.

'Why the hurry?' asked Orlo.

'Welllll,' drawled the Doctor. 'For one thing, I want to see how quickly its intelligence develops. And two…' He peered at something over Ty and Orlo's shoulders, down the slope.

They turned – to see a carpet of writhing, wriggling brown bodies, flashing silver where the sunlight reflected from their still-wet fur, making its way up the bank from the river. Towards them.

Ty looked back at the Doctor. He raised an eyebrow.

'How's that for two?'

The three of them ran like they'd never run before – or at least like *Ty* had never run before.

Puffing and panting, her feet slipping on the muddy grass, she got the impression that the Doctor was holding himself back for her and Orlo's sakes. He'd snatched the otter from the boy to make it a bit easier for him, and didn't even break his stride.

'Grab my jacket!' he said as they ran along the slope, parallel to the river – the quickest way back to the settlement. Ahead of them, down along the edge of the water, Ty could see the remains of the old city, poking through like a misshapen skeleton. The level had dropped even further in the last hour and a half hour.

She grabbed the jacket from where it was hooked over the crook of his arm.

'Inside pocket,' he said. 'Other one – that's it. No, not that!' Ty had pulled out the black wallet with his mysteriously versatile business card. 'Not unless you think I can persuade them that I'm Doctor Dolittle.'

'Dolittle?' puffed Ty. 'Is *that* your name?'

The Doctor ignored her question. 'The other pocket, Ty!' He glanced back at the swarm of otters, galloping after them. 'The other one!'

With the jacket flailing around in her hands as she ran, she managed to reach in and pull out the first thing she found: the torch that he'd used on the creature in the otter nest.

'This?'

'At last.' He stopped dead and held out the now-snoring otter to Orlo. 'Take it and go, both of you. Get back to the settlement. Tell them what we've seen.'

Ty just stared at him, at the brown and silver tide flowing along the ground towards them, and then at Orlo.

'*Go!*' he shouted.

Ty squeezed his arm and, with a single, helpless look back, she grabbed Orlo and the two of them ran.

'Now,' muttered the Doctor to himself, whirling to face the oncoming storm. 'Let's just hope your hearing is as sensitive as I hope it is.' He remembered how the otter in the cage had flinched – and that was when he'd just been using the sonic screwdriver as a torch.

He raised it and held it out in front of him. 'Otherwise it's going to get a whole lot hotter for me.' He paused and raised his eyebrows appreciatively. 'Hotter. *Otter*. Oooh, that's quite good. I might use that one later.' He narrowed his eyes. 'When I've got a more appreciative audience. Sorry little fellers – this is going to hurt you a whole lot more than it does me.'

And with that, he pressed the button.

For a moment, nothing happened. The living carpet of scampering otters continued to race towards him at terrifying speed, the sunlight glittering in their obsidian eyes, their teeth bared. Even the Doctor winced at the wave of ultrasound emanating from the screwdriver, and he stuck one finger in his ear, uselessly.

And then the otters began to react.

The ones at the leading edge of the attack skidded to a messy, tumbling halt, some of them falling bum-over-head in their haste. The ones right behind them couldn't stop in time and went crashing into them. It was like they'd hit a glass wall. But still the ones behind came. More and more of them began to pile up, writhing around, squeaking at the tops of their voices.

'Sorry,' whispered the Doctor, but he continued to hold the button down, and watched as the otters piled up in a huge arc a couple of hundred feet away from him.

He gave it another five seconds – until the stragglers had reached the front, climbing up onto the rapidly growing mound of writhing brown bodies, where they too felt the screwdriver's ultrasonic waves enough to start screeching. Still gripping it firmly, he turned his head to see where the two of them were. Ty and Col were just tiny figures in the distance, rounding the gentle swell of headland where the first settlement had been built. Even as he watched, they paused, looked back at him one last time, and then vanished.

'That should just about do it,' he said to himself, and lowered the screwdriver.

The otters continued to shriek and chatter and roll around, clambering over each other like a litter of newborn kittens.

Slipping the sonic screwdriver into his trouser pocket, he set off at a sprint after Ty and Orlo.

The ship smelled horribly of rust and mildew and old fish. In fact, as Candy hoisted herself into the airlock, she saw a dead, half-rotted one on the floor and kicked it out of the door. The gridded metal beneath her feet was slippery with algae, but at least it meant she could see where Col's boots had been – it looked like he'd headed towards the flight deck, the ship's main control room.

There was something eerie about the *One Small Step* now, not least because the light was fading rapidly outside, as it did on Sunday. But mainly because it was just *so* quiet. When the settlers had boarded, back on Earth, the ship had been humming and buzzing with power and electronics and people. Even after they'd landed and unloaded all their stuff, even after they'd set up Sunday City, the ship had been left on low power, just to keep all the computer systems ticking over. It was where she and Orlo had come to learn Morse code, to play games against the shipbrain, to mess about.

But now it was like a haunted house. The only sound was a distant drip-drip-drip of water and the occasional creak or groan from the vessel's rusted fabric. Candy found herself holding her breath without realising it, and felt a sudden need to call out to Col, to find him, give him a hug.

And then get the hell off the ship.

Although there was no power for the lifts, there were tube-ladders alongside them all. It was getting dark now, so Candy pulled out her torch, steeled herself, and headed up towards the flight deck. As she heaved herself into the central passageway she could see dim, flickering light from up ahead. Col must be there.

Her foot clanged dully on the floor as she took a step forward.

'Col?' she called, wondering why there was no noise from up ahead. Something metallic and echoey sounded behind her, away down the passage, and she jumped. But the trembling light from her torch showed her nothing. She turned back and continued her way towards the prow of the ship. Fortunately, the vessel was only leaning at a slight angle, otherwise she'd have had to walk along the walls and jump over the open doors.

'Col!' she called again, louder, as she approached the entrance to the flight deck. 'It's me – Candy! You there?'

Taking a deep breath, she gripped the edge of the door frame and pulled herself in. The room was bathed in deep orange light from the sinking sun, washing over everything. But it cast shadows over some of the computer consoles where she could see lights flickering and winking. Col must have got the power going. So where was he?

'Col!' she hissed as loudly as she dared, gripping the torch like a gun. Above her she could see that the other main window was shattered too. A plant creeper or something had grown in through it.

Candy almost jumped out of her skin as a cracked, broken voice whispered her name, and she swung the torch in its direction.

Lying on the floor, half-concealed by a desk, was Col – staring up at her with coal-black eyes.

The Doctor paused to catch his breath only once he was at the old settlement, more than a little disappointed that he hadn't had a chance to check out the settlers' ship – but that could wait.

He glanced back, briefly, at the top of the rise. The pile of otters, like a huge, chocolate sand dune, was slowly disentangling itself and spreading out – spreading out back to the water. Either they'd been scared off by the ultrasound, or they'd decided that it wasn't worth chasing him. Of course, he mused, it could be that they'd prioritised the dismantling of the dam. He glanced up to see that clouds were once more gathering. He hadn't thought to borrow an umbrella, either.

Were the otters acting on instinct, or with intelligence? Attack as a means of defence could be either. Or both.

But they'd only attacked when Ty had shot the otter. Most animals would take flight if they saw that happen. Most animals acting on instinct, at least.

He knew he had to get back to the zoo lab fairly quickly and take a closer look at their new little friend – have a poke about, see what was making it tick. But he couldn't resist taking another look at the remains of the first Sunday City before he went.

It was certainly more impressive than the collection of log cabins they'd cobbled together since the flood. Many of the buildings were plastic prefabs, although there were no signs of smart buildings amongst the soggy, weed-encrusted structures before him. A colony on the cheap, he knew – the fission generator had told him that. The river had receded so far that only half of the settlement still lay in the puddled water. The rest appeared to be sitting on smooth, brown mud flats, and the bottom two or three metres of most of the buildings looked like they'd been dipped in chocolate and left out to set.

At the thought of chocolate, the Doctor realised that he couldn't remember the last time he'd eaten. Breakfast was *well* overdue. He thought again of Martha. If he hadn't blithely assumed that she'd be safe in the TARDIS, she might be with him now, marvelling at all of this, instead of lying in a hospital bed. That was one of the things he loved about Martha: her ability to get excited by anything and everything. The universe was still a source of wonder to her. Every time she stepped out of the TARDIS there was a childlike glee in her eyes. Sometimes he wondered whether that wasn't part of the reason he didn't like to travel alone. Nine hundred years of scooting about the universe could make you jaded to its delights. And seeing them anew, through the eyes of someone who'd never witnessed them before… It was, he imagined, why Christmas was such a wonderful time for adults. They could experience the joy of it all over again through their children's eyes.

Still, he consoled himself, Martha would be up and about before he knew it.

Now that the water had fallen further, he could see the tops of a few vehicles, further out into the river. Two that looked like huge mechanical diggers, something with a spiky bit on top and a couple of quad bikes, tipped over on their sides like dead insects. Now *they*, he thought, would be useful – not to mention fun. Save all this running around everywhere. He doubted that they'd work without a good servicing, though.

Suddenly, a sliver of movement caught his eye. An otter darted splashily out of the water onto the mud and scampered across it, leaving a trail of tiny paw prints. It ignored him, and headed straight for a low, squat, grey building, flat-roofed and with a single small window on the side facing him.

The otter was followed, within seconds, by another. And then another.

He didn't like the look of this. For a start, he'd just been chased across the countryside by thousands of their chums, and there could well be thousands more swimming upriver at this very moment. They may even have worked out that swimming would get them to him faster than running. But he was intrigued by the purposefulness of their behaviour. They weren't just sniffing around to see what was what – they were heading for one very specific building.

Perhaps that was a food store and they could smell the goodies in there. Although, after all this time, any food in there would surely have rotted or been washed away by the flood.

Whatever the reason for their interest in that particular building, it was a puzzle that would have to wait a while. With one last look back, he set off up the hill.

Col gazed at Candy blankly. In the dim light, it looked as though his pupils had dilated fully, engulfing his irises. Blue eyes, she remembered. Col had the palest blue eyes – a legacy from his Irish ancestors. And now they were just black.

'Col!' hissed Candy wanting to go to him, but scared to move. 'It's me – Candy!'

Col's expression didn't change, but he blinked slowly, like a hungry insect.

'What's happened?' Candy continued.

'Candy…' Col's voice was a low murmur, almost inaudible. He raised a hand, weakly, as if to push her back.

'In my head,' he whispered. 'It's in my head.' His lip trembled, but his eyes stayed fixed, emotionless.

Candy felt herself panicking: what was he talking about? Had he slipped and hurt himself?

'It's all right, Col. Let's get you back to—'

Col blinked, slow and insectile again, and raised his

hand.

'Stay back,' he said. 'It's not safe… not safe here.' He paused and blinked again. 'It's looking for things,' he said softly. 'In my head. It's… It's trying to learn.'

'Learn what? What's in your head, Col?' She dropped to her knees. 'C'mon, Col. Please… let's go, let's get out of here.'

There was another long pause.

'We have things that it doesn't… It wants to use us.'

'Stop it, Col, you're scaring me!'

Col gave a long sigh and his body jerked as if electrified. His mouth twitched a faint, almost curious smile.

'Intelligence. It wants our intelligence… It *needs* it.'

Candy didn't understand.

'What does it want to know?'

'No… no… It doesn't want to know *things*,' he said, his voice distant. 'It just wants to *know*. It needs intelligence.' He paused again, and a dreamy, faraway look spread across his face, despite the expressionless eyes. 'It's so *strange*, Candy.'

The torch almost slipped from Candy's sweating hand, and, for a moment, Col's face was swallowed up by the darkness.

'Are you hurt?' she asked as she found him again, still not quite understanding why Col wasn't moving – or why she wasn't trying to move him.

'No pain,' Col murmured. 'Strange that, eh?' A weird smile cracked his face. Candy wondered if he'd been taking drugs or something – something he'd found on the ship. Was *that* why he'd been so keen to come back here?

'Well you can tell the Doctor about it later, when we get back. Can you move? Can you sit up?'

Col gave another sigh and then, as if the urgency of the situation had finally sunk in, placed the flat of his palm against the floor and tried to push himself upright. He managed a few inches.

'What's that?' Candy whispered.

There was something behind Col, something that had been hidden when he'd been lying down. It looked like black rope, a couple of inches across, dangling from the back of Col's neck down to the floor.

'What?'

'Behind you, on your neck. Look, just move over here – we can worry about that later.'

Col forced himself up into a sitting position, his legs bent sideways, blocking Candy's view of whatever it was. He reached behind his head with his free hand – and a look of puzzlement, and then fear, swept across his face.

'What is it?' Candy asked.

For a few seconds, Col said nothing as he felt around behind him. And then, as if wanting to show Candy, he turned his head sideways.

Attached to the back of Col's head, just above the nape of the neck, was the rope. Only it wasn't rope: in the torchlight it was glossy and wet. And then Candy realised that it led to the shattered window. It was the creeper that she'd seen as she'd arrived.

But the worst, most horrible thing, was that it was pulsing, very gently, as though pumping fluids. Into Col's head. She saw his fingers splayed out around, where it joined his flesh.

'What's happened?' His voice was low and cold and fearful. 'What's happened?'

'It's OK, Col,' Candy managed to say, feeling the sick rising in her throat. She swallowed it back. 'Just move over here and we'll have a look at it. We'll get it off.'

But Col didn't move. She watched his fingers probe and explore the interface between him and the thing.

Suddenly, his body jerked and his hands fell by his sides. Candy dropped the torch and, panicked, hunted around for it with her hands, her eyes never leaving Col's silhouette.

'It's learning,' he said, and blinked. As she found the torch and brought it back up to his face, she saw that the whites of his eyes looked darker now, greener. Maybe it was just the light. Maybe.

'Go, Candy – get away. Tell the Doctor—' He broke off as his body arched, like he'd been given an electric shock.

'I'm not leaving you,' she said firmly.

'It wants to use us. It wants us to be—' Again he stopped, his head tipped back, mouth open. 'I can't stop it, Candy. It's flicking through my head like a book. Oh…' Col paused, a frown etched onto his face.

Candy didn't know what to do. She couldn't leave but she was terrified of staying.

'Col!' she hissed again. 'You've got to help me – move over here and—'

'It's too late,' he said with a slow, painful exhalation of breath. 'Too late.'

'It's *not!*' Candy almost shouted. She didn't understand quite what was going on, what the thing was doing with Col, but she knew that Col was still there. And if he was still there, then she had to do *something*.

'Tell them I'm sorry,' he said, lowering his eyes until he was staring straight at her.

'For what?'

'For letting it find out.'

'Find out about what? Col, what are you talking about?'

'Pallister,' Col said, a look of intense sadness on his face. 'Pallister's who it needs. Oh Candy… what have I—'

'Forget Pallister. Col, we've got to get out of here.'

But Col stayed where he was. Slowly, painfully, as if every movement was agony, he reached back behind his head with both hands.

'I'm sorry,' he said again. 'Tell them I couldn't help it. Tell them.'

And then he gritted his teeth and closed his eyes.

Only then did Candy realise what he was going to do – and that it was too late to stop him.

She didn't close her eyes quickly enough to block out the sight of Col wrenching the vile, alien tendril from the back of his head; not quickly enough to prevent her seeing the spray of glutinous ichor that poured out of the severed end; and not quickly enough to miss the look of peace and serenity that passed across his face just before he died.

EIGHT

The Doctor arrived back at the zoo lab to find Ty and Orlo fastening the cage door on their newest recruit.

'Doctor!' cried Ty with relief, flinging herself at him and giving him a huge bear hug.

'Numbers eight and… nine,' he managed to gasp.

'Eight and nine what?' she said, letting him go.

'Ribs – that you've just broken,' the Doctor gasped, rubbing his sides.

Ty began to apologise, but he just grinned and waved her away.

'They'll heal. Now we've got work to do. How is he?' He gestured at the otter, still snoring away.

'Seems fine – should be coming round in about half an hour.'

'Good, good,' the Doctor said thoughtfully. 'Now – this…' He quickly grabbed a pen and a piece of paper from the desk and began scribbling. '… is what I need, equipment-wise. Think you can rustle this up for me? Or at least point me in the right direction.'

He shoved the paper into Ty's hand and strode over to inspect the new otter.

'We've got to work fast,' he said. 'The otters are demonstrating if not intelligence, then distinctly purposeful behaviour. We already have that—' He indicated the scratched outline of his ship on the wall '—to prove that they're aware of the TARDIS. And I've just seen them going into one of the exposed buildings from the first settlements. A whole cartload of them – cartload? Is that the word? What's the collective noun for otters?' He clicked his fingers in the air repeatedly and then beamed a huge grin. '*Romp!* That's the word. Romp! Well,' he added, 'one of them at least – but certainly my favourite. Isn't that lovely? "A romp of otters".'

He stared at their blank faces.

'Please yourselves. Anyway,' he turned and addressed the otter. 'We've got to have a good look at you. How you getting on with the list, Ty?'

She scratched her head.

'What's a "planar thesiogram"? And this one...' She pointed with a finger. 'A "follengular beam... beamcaster"?'

She looked up at him.

'Oh that?' said the Doctor, looking slightly guilty. 'Scuse my handwriting. Feeling a bit peckish... that's a "full English breakfast". First of all, though, I need to check on Martha.'

'Are these really necessary?' demanded the Doctor, pointing at the leather restraints that fastened Martha's wrists and ankles to the bed. He couldn't bear to see anyone shackled or tied down, let alone Martha. In her sleep, she growled and thrashed her head from side to side. Her face was slick with sweat.

'It's for her own safety as much as anyone else's,' Sam Hashmi said apologetically. 'She was…' he stumbled for words.

'Like an animal?' suggested the Doctor.

Sam nodded.

The Doctor shook his head. He'd brought Martha to Sunday and he should have taken better care of her. If only he'd gone straight back to find the TARDIS instead of messing around in the zoo lab, this might never have happened. Sometimes he got caught up in things so much that he forgot there were other people around, other people that he cared about.

He leaned over Martha and stroked her forehead with the backs of his fingers. She flinched, her body arched up from the bed, and then collapsed back.

'What medication have you given her?' he asked Sam without looking up.

'Antipyretics to bring her fever down and some broad-spectrum antibiotics to help counter any infection.' He didn't sound hopeful.

The Doctor leaned back and looked up at the display above Martha's bed. For a few moments, he scanned it, taking in all the readings. There was something he was missing, he felt sure of it. Something not quite right…

'It's not an infection,' he said suddenly, more to himself

than to Sam.

'It's not?'

He shook his head.

'It's an allergic reaction – look at those readings. What are her histamine levels?'

Sam fumbled about with the clipboard for a moment.

'You're right,' he said, almost disbelievingly. 'And it's on a massive scale!'

'She's close to anaphylactic shock – we need adrenaline or epinephrine or whatever you're calling it these days.'

'I'm on it.'

Sam rushed off to get the drug whilst the Doctor continued to calm Martha down.

'Don't you worry, Martha Jones,' he whispered. 'We're going to pull you through this. And then we're going to *Tiffany's* for that breakfast I promised you. And you know how seriously I take promises.'

He tried to sound positive, knowing that somewhere under the fever Martha would be hearing his words. She seemed to relax for a few moments and her eyes opened blearily. There was no sign of her brown irises, just black holes sunk into the dull green of her corneas.

'Martha,' whispered the Doctor, 'can you hear me?'

She gave a little moan and stared at him with those cold, alien eyes.

'Too dry,' she murmured.

'What is?'

'Too dry,' she repeated, as if she hadn't heard him. 'Must go back… back to the water… Must go…'

She closed her eyes and sank back into the damp pillow.

'Why?' urged the Doctor. 'Why have you got to go?'

But Martha didn't answer. She just moaned quietly, flexing her wrists against the straps.

'Here we are,' said Sam suddenly, gently elbowing the Doctor out of the way. In his hand he held a syringe. The Doctor could only hope that, although the adrenaline might reduce Martha's body's response to whatever was inside her, it wouldn't get rid of it.

'It might take a while to kick in,' Sam said, stepping back from the bed.

The Doctor nodded and squeezed Martha's hand, his eyes scanning the monitor. But even as he watched, he could see that the adrenaline was working. Martha's breathing became less laboured, less painful. He watched her for a few minutes. There was nothing more he could do for her now that the drug was starting to work – but there *was* something he had to find out.

'Take care of her,' he said to Sam. 'let me know when she comes round.'

And with a last look back at his friend, the Doctor headed for the zoo lab.

Unfortunately, before he could get down to the work of examining the new otter, the Doctor discovered that he had another problem to deal with.

Making his way across the square, he saw an officious little figure come bustling out of the Council building towards him. He really didn't have time for Pallister.

But Pallister was not in the mood to be ignored.

'Doctor!' he called across the square. The Doctor pretended he hadn't seen or heard him, and carried on walking. But Pallister sped up.

'Doctor,' he said from too close for the Doctor to carry on his act. He spun round and smiled brightly. It often disarmed people, he thought – although one look at Pallister's grim face suggested that this wasn't going to be one of those occasions.

'Ahh,' he said. 'Mr Lassiter.'

'Pallister,' the man corrected him, and the Doctor saw the angry twitch of a muscle at the corner of the Chief Councillor's mouth.

'How can I help you? I'm rather busy at the moment.'

'There's a Council meeting this evening,' Pallister said, clasping his hands together. 'I'd like to know what I can tell them about your presence here.'

'Of course you would. Well, as soon as I find out, you'll be the first to know.'

Pallister was thrown.

'You don't know why you're here?'

'Oh, I know why I'm here.' The Doctor leaned closer, his voice dropping to a conspiratorial whisper. '*Trouble*,' he said simply.

'Trouble? What sort of trouble?'

The Doctor looked around, as if they might be overheard.

'The *worst* kind of trouble, if you take my meaning.'

'And, erm, what would that be, exactly?'

'There's something bad going on here, Mr Pallister. Something very bad indeed – and I'm going to get to the bottom of it.' He paused again for effect. 'It's what I do.'

With that, he clasped Pallister's clammy little hand firmly, gave it a shake, and rushed off to the zoo lab, leaving Sunday's Chief Councillor standing, dumbfounded, in the middle of the square.

The Doctor was quite impressed at the level of technology that the Sundayans had managed to salvage from the flood. He was less impressed with the breakfast. He was still picking bits of what they laughingly called tomatoes out of his teeth as he carried the otter to the examining table and swung the huge lamp into position over his head.

He held out his hand, palm up, to one side.

'Swab,' he said sternly.

'What?' Ty stared at him.

'Sorry. Getting carried away there. Just pass those scissors, will you?'

Ty's stare became wider.

'Just a little short back and sides,' he explained.

Ty handed him the scissors and he set about clipping the hair around the otter's ears.

'Well, sir,' he said in a cheery tone of voice. 'Going anywhere nice for your holidays? Really? Lovely! See the game last night?' He snipped and tutted, rolling his eyes. 'We were robbed, weren't we, eh? That last-minute penalty, eh?'

'What *are* you on about?' said Ty, helping to pick away the tufts of the otter's hair as the Doctor reached the skin.

'Hairdresser's banter,' grinned the Doctor. He paused and squinted at his handiwork. 'He's not going to be too happy with *that* when he comes round. Never mind – a bit of gel'll sort it out. Maybe some extensions. Oooh, there we are: look!'

Ty peered closer: speckling the surface of the skin, in a broad band across its head, stretching from ear to ear, were tiny, dark-red dots.

'It's the same as on Martha, isn't it? What are you doing?'

The Doctor picked up a syringe and handed it to Ty.

'Like to do the honours? Cerebrospinal fluid, please – five millilitres.'

Ty took the syringe, tipped the otter's head to one side, carefully inserted the tip of the needle into the back of its neck and began to withdraw the plunger. The syringe filled up with a brownish-pink fluid.

'What are we looking for?'

'I'll tell you that when we've found it. Right!' He took the syringe from Ty and held it up to the light. 'Let's get this over to the bio lab – I've got a feeling this might be just the breakthrough we need.'

'It's incredible,' said Ty, her eyes scanning the screen set into the large, glossy desktop.

The bio lab, situated on the other side of the square, was a considerably more impressive building than the zoo lab. The settlers had been lucky that all this hadn't been lost in the flood too – although it couldn't begin to make up for the lost settlers themselves. On the outside, it looked much the same as the other buildings – a single-storey log cabin. But inside the walls had been lined with smooth, white plastic sheeting, heat-sealed and brightly lit to create a series of rooms that resembled the inside of a fridge. Cool, clean and clinical, even the air smelled sterile.

Three or four white-coated technicians busied themselves at various pieces of equipment on the benches arrayed around the room. Along with the reassuring beeping and whirring of machinery, there was a low hum of air conditioning. At the centre of the room was a table the size of a barn door, its surface dark and glass-smooth with half a dozen big screens set into it and a host of touch-sensitive panels and buttons around them.

The Doctor peered over her shoulder at the full-colour, computer-augmented images that rotated on the desk.

'Proteins!' he said. 'Now why aren't I surprised?'

He reached into his pocket, pulled out his spectacles and put them on. 'Now… let's have a look…'

Almost elbowing Ty aside, he took a deep breath and began typing on the virtual keyboard, projected onto the glass surface of the table.

'I didn't know it could do that!' exclaimed Ty as a single small screen suddenly grew to take up most of the surface of the table.

'It can't,' said the Doctor without looking at her, adding in a whisper: 'But don't tell anyone – it'll invalidate the guarantee. Oooh – look at *that*! Now *that* is interesting.'

He stood back proudly and folded his arms.

The vast tabletop screen was filled with an assortment of

strange, clumpy shapes, rotating, swirling, joining up with each other and forming long chains before breaking apart and reforming.

'I feel like I'm back at nursery school with you, Doctor,' Ty said tiredly. 'But at a guess—'

'Oh, an *educated* guess, surely, Professor.'

She ignored his flattery. 'At a guess, I'd say we were looking at protein synthesis.' She glanced up at the Doctor for confirmation. He just raised an eyebrow. 'That,' she said, tracing a long, twisty thread, 'is RNA, yes? And it's controlling the manufacture of these proteins.' She reached out and dabbed at three or four other images.

'Go on,' the Doctor said approvingly. 'And what's RNA for?'

'Ribonucleic acid is involved in the replication of DNA, the chemical that codes for the construction of living organisms,' she said, as if she were quoting from a textbook.

'And what else has RNA been implicated in?'

Ty frowned, watching the kaleidoscope of images in front of her.

'Not memories, surely?' She looked up at him in disbelief. 'But that idea was discredited on Earth decades ago.'

'We're not *on* Earth any more, Toto,' the Doctor reminded her with a grin.

Ty didn't understand, but suspected the Doctor was taking the mickey out of her. She turned back to the display table.

'So… you're saying that these proteins and this RNA

contain *memories*? Those things in the otters' nests are implanting *memories* into the otters?'

'Not just memories,' the Doctor said gravely. 'And not just the otters. These are the results from Martha.'

Ty's eyes widened.

'But why? Is this connected with the otters' braininess?'

The Doctor took off his glasses and twirled them in his fingers.

'When you catch the otters, they're dim but violent, and after a couple of days they turn clever and friendly. These proteins are just what you'd need to stimulate aggression – and suppress intelligence.'

'So it's not that the otters are *actually* getting cleverer,' said Ty, struggling to keep up with the speed of his train of thought, 'but that they're just returning to their *normal* level of smartness? The proteins have been holding them back, and once they're gone…'

The Doctor nodded.

'In the meantime, they're creating an allergic reaction in Martha's body.' He pursed up his lips and narrowed his eyes. 'But as to *why*…'

He turned suddenly.

'The other skeletons that I heard you'd found: have they been given a good going-over?'

Ty nodded. 'They were all people who disappeared during the flood. Dental records are pretty clear.'

'Causes of death?'

'Impossible to tell from the skeletons – I assumed they drowned. But they all have holes in their chests or their heads – different sizes. Some the size of a fist, others just pinpricks.'

The Doctor chewed thoughtfully on the arm of his glasses.

'Sounds to me like someone's been experimenting. Someone. Or some*thing*.'

'Experimenting?'

'Experimenting with human bodies – working out how they work, how to get inside them.'

Out of the corner of his eye, he saw Ty hug her arms to herself tighter.

'We really could do with understanding *why*, what those slimy little pets of the otters are up to.' His eyes lit up and he grinned. 'You know what we need to decode the RNA and the proteins, don't you?'

Ty shook her head.

'What we need is the most advanced biological computer I can think of.'

'Here?' Ty scoffed. 'You're lucky we've got all *this* stuff. Where d'you think you're going to lay your hands on something like that?'

The Doctor raised an eyebrow and gave her one of those stares.

'You're looking at it,' he said.

'You're mad!' cried Ty, staring at the Doctor with wide eyes.

'One man's madness is another man's, erm, poison,' the Doctor replied. 'Say hello to the Doctor-o-tronic.'

'Exactly,' Ty reiterated. 'This stuff *is* poison. Look what it's done to Martha – and you're going to, what, inject it into yourself?'

The Doctor pressed his lips together and took Ty's hands in his. His skin felt strangely cool.

'If there was another choice…' he said gently. 'We need to know what those slime-things are putting into the otters – and into Martha. Your equipment here might be sophisticated, but it's not *that* sophisticated. This, however—' He tapped his temple '—is!'

Ty shook her head firmly.

'Use me,' she said suddenly, impulsively. 'Inject it into me.'

'Humans might be clever,' the Doctor smiled, 'but I'm *brilliant*! And at the moment, we need brilliance, not another person who needs strapping to a bed.'

'How d'you know it won't be *you* who gets strapped to the bed? What makes you so special, hmm?'

He looked at her for a few moments.

'We don't have time to discuss it. Ty, I'm Martha's best chance. I brought her here, I owe it to her.'

There was a heavy silence between them, punctuated only by the bleeps and bloops of the equipment in the lab. Eventually, realising that he wouldn't give in, Ty sighed.

'OK – what do we need to do?'

NINE

Martha woke up, drenched in sweat, her hospital gown and the bed sheets clinging to her. For a moment, she had no idea where she was: a dimly lit room, a lemony, timbery smell in her nostrils. And then it came back to her – everything.

'How are you feeling?'

Martha jumped as a figure appeared out of the gloom. A short, elderly Indian man, peering at her worriedly.

'Where's the Doctor?'

'*The* Doctor?' the man said – his name came to her from nowhere: Dr Hashmi. Sam. He shook his head. 'I'm not sure. D'you want me to find him?'

Hashmi glanced into the air above her, and Martha followed his gaze to see some sort of display screen, hanging over her head, showing an augmented view of her body with numerous winking lights and flickering patches on it.

'How am I?' she ventured.

Hashmi smiled cautiously.

'Your friend was right,' he said. 'We pumped you full of every antihistamine and epinephrine analogue we have and it seems to have done the trick. We've damped down your body's allergic reaction to whatever's inside you.'

Martha let out a sigh and gripped the edge of the sheets – but Hashmi placed his hand on hers before she could throw them back. He'd taken the restraints off when he'd seen that she was no longer dangerous.

'But I think you should have a bit more rest. Your body's very weak – we've had to feed you intravenously.'

For the first time, Martha noticed the tube taped to the back of her wrist.

'I've got to find the Doctor,' she said.

'I'll find him for you. Stay here and I'll get you something to eat and drink. If you get up now, you'll be back in bed in minutes, trust me. You've had quite a shock.'

Martha pursed her lips.

'OK,' she said, folding her hands on her stomach. 'You find him, I'll stay here.'

He nodded. 'Give me ten minutes,' he said before disappearing.

Martha gave him five, and then she was out of bed, pulling the IV tube from her hand with a wince and smoothing the surgical tape back over it. Out of bed, and feeling decidedly weak and wobbly, she rooted around in the bedside cabinet for her clothes, but there was nothing. They must have taken them away to clean them. She scanned the ward. She was the only patient, so there were no other clothes she could steal. If she'd been back in the Royal Hope and any of her patients had behaved like this, the staff would have screamed blue murder at them. But she wasn't, and this was different, she told herself.

Keeping an ear and an eye out for any other staff, Martha padded to the far end of the ward in her bare feet and found a locker containing a couple of slightly tatty dressing gowns. Slipping one on, she caught sight of her reflection in the mirror above a hand basin: she looked tired and drawn and there were huge bags under her eyes. She was sure she'd lost some weight – and not in a good way. Her normally perfect hair was lank and flopped down over her forehead. She half-heartedly pushed it back, but it just dropped down again.

Never mind. She had to find the Doctor. The locker contained some horrid, rough sandal-type slippers. A bit small for her. They'd do.

Checking again to make sure no one had seen her, Martha tightened the belt on the dressing gown and headed out into the night. The twilight was falling, but the air was pleasantly cool after the afternoon shower, and everything smelled of summer and holidays abroad.

Martha slipped out of the hospital and found herself in the middle of some sort of town square, paved with huge, flat sheets of what looked like shiny concrete. It was bordered by low, wooden buildings, and she remembered the view she'd had from the hospital earlier in the day. With dim sodium lights flickering on between the buildings, it confirmed her impression of a holiday camp.

There were few people about, and most of the windows were dark.

A couple strolled out from between two buildings, arm in arm, whispering into each other's shoulders, and Martha shrunk back into the shadow of the hospital. She had no idea where to go, where the Doctor was – where *anyone* was. She should have stayed in bed, let Dr Hashmi find the Doctor and bring him to her. This was just stupid.

Think it through, she told herself. *Where would he be? It would have to be something important to keep him away from her bedside, wouldn't it?*

Martha let her gaze drift around the square. There was nothing to indicate what the buildings were. For all she knew, they were all offices, empty and deserted at this time of the day.

Something moved in the darkness at the base of one of the buildings on the other side of the square: small, lithe shapes, slipping through the shadows like fish through water. A chill trickled down her spine as she recognised something familiar in their movements. *Otters*, she thought.

As she watched, and her eyes became accustomed to the darkness, she could see that there were dozens of them, silently flitting between the buildings. And at least one of those buildings still had lights on. If that was where the Doctor was, she had to warn him.

Pallister allowed a grin to creep across his face.

His earlier annoyance that the Doctor, despite his promise, had not been to see him was almost forgotten in his joy at how absurdly easy the Council had been to manipulate. It was as if they'd left all their critical faculties, all their judgement, back on Earth.

The flood, whilst obviously disastrous for the settlement, hadn't been without its upside: eight members of the Council had been lost that night, and the replacement members had been, at the very least, reluctant. So reluctant, so scared of exercising any power, that they'd been almost pathetically grateful to Pallister for taking charge.

Sunday needed firm government, Pallister had reminded himself, every day since the catastrophe. It needed someone capable of making harsh decisions, someone not scared of being unpopular. And if there was one thing that Pallister had never been scared of, it had been that. And, fortunately, he'd had an ally in that, someone who'd seen the strength of leadership he could provide. He wondered, briefly, where Col was and why he hadn't heard from him about his trip to the ship. It must have gone OK, otherwise Col would have been back to tell him. Never mind – there were more important things to sort out now.

He'd almost had to laugh at the panic and confusion in their eyes – especially in the eyes of that stupid woman Marj Haddon – when he'd told them that an adjudicator had been sent from Earth.

'Why?' she'd bleated, going even paler than she normally was. 'The flood?'

Pallister just shrugged, trying to give the subtle impression that he knew more than he was letting on.

'But why have they sent an *adjudicator*?' This was Dory Chan – one of the few Councillors to have challenged any of Pallister's recent suggestions. She had a hard face and disturbingly penetrating eyes. 'And why didn't he make himself known to us all?'

'He made himself known to *me*,' Pallister pointed out gently, omitting the fact that it had been *he* that had had gone to the Doctor. 'As for why…'

He let the silence hang for a while, knowing that almost all the Councillors (except, perhaps, Chan) would be desperately wondering whether they'd done something wrong – some silly little infringement of the Council rules, some stupid mess-up in protocol. And then, when he'd let them panic enough, he said: 'I'll handle the Doctor.'

The sighs of relief were audible.

But Chan wasn't quite so ready to hand over responsibility to Pallister. She brushed her black hair back over her ear and coughed pointedly.

'Would it not be a good idea,' she ventured, an edge to her voice, 'for the Doctor to meet with us? *All* of us? And if he knows something about the ship… I take it you've sent someone out to investigate? To check that he's not lying?'

Pallister spread his hands.

'It's all in hand, Councillor Chan. And I would agree with you about us all meeting with him, but adjudicators are a law unto themselves, as I'm sure you know. To demand his attendance here might just antagonise him further.'

'What d'you mean, "further"? As far as I can tell, we've not antagonised him at all yet—'

Chan stopped and frowned, glancing around the Council.

'What's that noise?'

Pallister listened hard.

From somewhere, somewhere in the walls of the building, he could hear scratching noises. Tiny, almost inaudible scratching noises.

Pallister tapped at the intercom in front of him.

'Eton,' he snapped to his aide, waiting in the outer office. 'What's that noise?'

'Noise, Councillor?' came back Eton's tinny voice. 'I…'

Eton's voice suddenly cut off with a sharp thump.

'Eton?' barked Pallister, stabbing at the button again. 'Eton!'

There was no reply. But from the intercom came a chittering and squeaking.

'Eton?'

Pallister pulled the door to the outer office open sharply, not quite sure what he expected to see. Behind him were the rest of the Councillors, puzzled and confused.

The office was empty, the chair behind the desk lying on its side.

'What's happened?' asked Marj Haddon, pushing past him. 'Where's Eton?'

The front door was open, and she crossed to it, peering out into the night. The square was silent and deserted.

'Listen!' hissed Chan, and Marj turned suddenly.

They could all hear it now: a frantic scrabbling and scratching, an animal noise from behind the walls and under the floors. Nervously, the Councillors began to back into the chamber, muttering amongst themselves.

'Oh God…'

It was Chan: she was staring into the shadows under the tables and cabinets around the Council chamber. Shadows that were moving; shadows that slid out from under the furniture and into the room, raising themselves up.

All around them, their eyes glinting as they opened their mouths to show their teeth, were dozens and dozens of otters.

'What… what do they want?' whispered Chan, drawing back and bumping into the tight little clot of Councillors that had formed in the doorway.

'They don't "want" anything,' snapped Pallister, trying hard to stamp down the edge of fear in his own voice. 'They're animals.'

'Why are they here?' someone else asked.

'Didn't they take the adjudicator's friend to one of their nests?' asked another, his voice trembling. 'Didn't they?'

The otters were silent and motionless, up on their back legs, front paws hanging down as they watched the Councillors.

'Food!' hissed Marj. 'They want us for food!'

'They're vegetarians,' Pallister said.

'So Ty says,' retorted Chan, clearly unconvinced.

Pallister tried to ignore their frightened mutterings and calmed himself with steady breathing, despite the hammering of his heart. He couldn't have gone through the flood, the reconstruction and the struggle to get himself to the top of the food chain around here only for it to end like this. He wouldn't allow it. He understood that the otters were clever. Not intelligent, but clever. So their behaviour had to have a purpose. And one of them had to be the leader, the head of the pack, the Alpha Male – whatever. He scanned the higgledy-piggledy ranks of animals, looking for a sign, anything that might give him a clue.

He coughed and cleared his throat.

'What do you want?' he asked loudly.

'What are you—'

'We mean you no harm,' Pallister interrupted Chan, addressing the nearest otter. Its ears twitched, but it showed no sign of understanding his words.

'Pallister,' Chan continued. 'They're *animals* – you've just said so.'

'Shut up!' he barked, turning his head sideways.

It was as though that were a signal. In an instant, the otters dropped to all fours, and began to advance on the Councillors.

Her slippers pinching her feet, Martha ran up the wooden steps and straight through the double doors of the building. Standing in a small reception room, talking to a small, red-haired woman behind a curved desk, was Sam Hashmi.

'Where is he?' Martha snapped.

Sam turned, hands raised as if to pacify her.

'Martha, wait,' he said.

She ignored him, pushing his hands away and casting round for some clue as to where the Doctor might be. Another set of double doors was straight ahead of her.

'You can't go in there,' Sam called, but Martha ignored

him. Out of the corner of her eye, she saw him coming after her, but raced on through the doors, letting them flap back in his face.

'Martha!' he called. 'You can't—'

He broke off as Martha reached a door on her left, a circular glass porthole set in it. She almost skidded to a halt and pressed her palms against the door.

'Oh God!' she whispered hoarsely, shaking her head. 'No, no…'

Almost in a trance, Martha pushed on the doors and stepped into the room.

Two people were standing by a bed – a bed lit by a single spotlight from above. A bed occupied by a single patient, strapped down at the wrists and ankles. A patient who was thrashing about, growling like an animal and grunting horribly.

Almost magically, the people by the bed moved back as Martha approached.

'Oh Doctor,' Martha moaned.

At the sound of her voice, the Doctor threw his head up, his pale, sweaty face shining like a full moon in the light. His teeth were bared and his lips were wet with saliva, dripping down his chin onto his shirt.

His eyes flashed open – they were totally dark. A greeny-black sheen swirled across them like oil, rainbow patterns reflected back from the lamp.

'You,' he grunted, more spittle flying from his lips. 'All of you. Will… be… ME!'

TEN

'What have you done?' cried Martha, raising a hand towards the Doctor as he continued to growl and snarl. The bed rattled as he tugged at the wrist straps. He stared at her with those dead, dark eyes and something pulled his lips into a vicious parody of a smile.

'Honey, he wanted to do it,' said a woman – a big black woman with braided hair – who Martha vaguely recognised.

'Do what?'

'He said it was the only way.'

The woman reached out to take Martha's hand but she pushed it away angrily, unable to take her eyes off her friend. He suddenly collapsed back onto the bed, moaning gently as his eyelids closed.

'The only way to *what*? He's let that thing touch him, hasn't he?'

'Thing?'

'In the otters' nest – he's gone there and—'

'No,' the woman said firmly, causing Martha to look at her properly for the first time. 'No, he hasn't. He had us inject him with the same proteins and RNA that the "thing" injected into you.'

'What? You're mad,' Martha spat. 'All of you – you're mad! You saw what it did to me and you *let* him?'

'He seems to know what he's doing,' a small, pale man in a lab coat said, clearly trying to be reassuring. It didn't work.

The Doctor growled and hissed again, his eyes flashing darkly as if they had the power to devour them all. Martha's shoulders sagged and she stared at him, pinned out on the bed like a live lab rat about to be dissected. Why had he done it? What could he possibly hope to gain?

'His body's fighting it,' the woman said gently.

Martha rounded on her, riled by her calm and reasonable tone of voice.

'And what if it doesn't?'

'Yours did,' the woman pointed out.

'But he's not like us. He's not…' Martha faltered, suddenly unsure of what the Doctor might have told them about himself. *He's not human.* She couldn't tell them that. Here she was again, thrown into the middle of a situation she knew nothing about.

'Who are you, anyway?' she asked the woman.

'Ty – Ty Benson. I visited you in the hospital.' She looked back at the Doctor, as if drawing a comparison. 'I heard about what happened – about you attacking Sam and Carolina.'

Martha looked back at the bed. Was the same thing

happening to the Doctor? She knew he was strong, knew that he wasn't human – but what if that made him *more* susceptible to the slime-thing? Martha had seen him possessed by a living sun – and survive. What did she really know about him, about what he was capable of, about his weaknesses? She reached out a hand to his forehead, but his head snapped up and he tried to bite her, smiling slyly when he failed.

'Martha,' Ty said in a very serious voice. 'How much do you know about him – the Doctor?'

'What d'you mean?' She couldn't take her eyes off the Doctor. He'd relaxed back onto the bed, but his face was still flushed and his chest rose and fell raggedly.

Ty gestured to a display panel hanging above the Doctor, much like the one that had been over her own bed. It showed the pale blue outline of a body, numerous patches of colour and flashing dots around it and on it. And pulsing on the chest there were two reddish circles, one over each lung. They flashed alternately.

'He has two hearts,' Ty said.

'Oh,' said Martha, trying not to look as if she were frantically thinking of what to say. 'Yeah.'

'*Two hearts*,' repeated Ty, clearly making some sort of point.

Suddenly there was a scream from the reception area and a loud, indecipherable shout. The doors slammed open and the red-haired receptionist rushed in, her face pale.

'They're out there – in reception,' she stammered. 'Otters.'

Martha realised, with a flash of guilt, that seeing the Doctor here had driven all thoughts of the otters from her head.

'Lock the door!' Martha shouted. 'Block it with something!'

Martha rushed to the double doors and grabbed the handles, just as they began to shake and rattle. In her panic, she almost let go. Ty joined her, and whilst they held the doors shut, the doctor in the white coat brought over a drip stand and pushed it through the handles, barring the door.

'Where else could they get in?' Martha demanded. 'Quick! C'mon!'

The doctor glanced through a door at the far side of the Doctor's bed, and darted over to shut and lock it.

'That's it?' said Martha, scanning the room. There were just the two doors – and a window, with heavy wooden shutters already closed.

Ty nodded and gave a start as the double doors, still barred, began to rattle ominously.

'What do they want?' she whispered. 'Why are they acting like this? They're *harmless*.'

'Yeah,' said Martha scathingly. 'Right.'

'No,' insisted Ty. 'They are. Normally, anyway.' She rubbed her eyes. 'It's those things – those slime-things. They've changed them, made them more aggressive.'

'Like they changed me and the Doctor,' Martha observed. She glanced at him again. He seemed to be sleeping, although his eyes flickered and darted about under his eyelids, and his hands clenched and unclenched.

'What about everyone else?' the redheaded receptionist said, her voice tiny and scared.

'If they've any sense,' Martha said, 'they'll have barricaded themselves in.' She thought for a moment. 'Do we have any weapons? Guns, anything like that?'

'We're in a biology laboratory, honey,' Ty said pointedly.

'Drugs, then – tranquillisers.'

'There's tranquillisers back in the zoo lab.'

'We'd need to get past the otters to get to them,' Martha said, pressing her lips firmly together.

'Wait!' Ty said suddenly, and rushed over to the side of the Doctor's bed where his jacket was draped over a chair. She began to root about in his pockets and produced the sonic screwdriver.

'His torch!' she said triumphantly.

'The sonic screwdriver?'

'He used it to keep them back when we were attacked before.'

For a second, Martha felt a pang of jealousy. Whilst she'd been out cold, the Doctor had been running around having adventures with this woman. She pushed her silly feelings aside.

'Good,' Martha said, snatching it from Ty. 'What setting did he have it on?'

'What what?'

'Setting,' repeated Martha, waving the screwdriver in her face. 'It's got about five billion of them. Use the wrong one and we could blow up half the town. Has he used it since then? Has anyone?'

Ty frowned but shook her head.

'Well,' said Martha, 'we'll just have to hope that it's been left on the same one.'

She advanced towards the door, the sonic screwdriver held out gingerly in front of her.

'You can't go out there on your own,' Ty said.

'I can move faster on my own,' Martha said, seeing the nervous faces around her. 'No offence. And I need you lot to look after the Doctor – right?'

Ty nodded. There was no argument from the others.

Martha looked at the doctor who stood with one hand on the end of the drip stand. It rattled as the otters battered against the door, and she could hear the sounds of scratching. 'On three,' she said in a low voice. 'One... two... three!'

Martha pressed the button as she reached 'two', and the tip of the screwdriver lit up with its reassuring blue glow. A high-pitched, teeth-irritating whine filled the room and the sound of scrabbling at the door abruptly ceased.

And on 'three', the nervous young doctor slid back the stand that held the doors shut.

Nothing happened – the doors shook slightly, but the expected inrush of otters didn't happen. Martha stepped forward, still holding the screwdriver out in front of her, and pushed tentatively at one of the doors with her foot. It moved out a few inches before hitting something, and then it was pushed back at her. There was the sound of squeaking and pattering feet from the corridor, and Martha pushed the door again, harder this time. It moved further and swung back without hitting anything.

She glanced back at the Doctor and then at Ty.

'Take care of him,' she said. 'I'm trusting you, yeah?'

'You can,' replied Ty as if Martha's words had been a challenge.

'Which one's the zoo lab?'

'Back to the square and then diagonally across to the right. The light'll be on and there's a sign by the door. The tranqs are in the white cabinet in the corner. There'll be a tranq gun with them.'

Martha took another look at the Doctor. With a brief nod and the tightest of smiles, she held out the sonic screwdriver in front of her and stepped into the corridor.

Ty, the doctor and the receptionist, barricaded the door the moment Martha had gone, and Ty dropped heavily into the chair by the Doctor's bed. She picked up a cloth from the table and wiped his sweaty forehead. In his sleep, he gave a guttural moan and his lips formed into a toothy sneer.

'She's got guts,' Ty said. 'I'll give her that. I can see why you're… such good friends.'

She shook her head and squeezed the Doctor's hand.

'You idiot,' she hissed. 'You stupid, stupid idiot. What are you playing at, eh? What if this stuff… what if it kills you? What then? Then we're all in the—'

'Hello,' interrupted the doctor thoughtfully, staring up at the screen over the bed. 'Look at that.'

Ty looked.

'What's happening?'

'His temperature's dropping. And his…' the doctor

frowned. 'Well, whatever he has in his blood that are doing the job of white blood cells. The count's falling like crazy.'

Ty's heart raced.

She gave a little yelp as the Doctor's hand suddenly gripped hers painfully, crushing her fingers. She looked down as his eyes flicked open. They were dark, like pools of tar. A cruel smile crossed his face again.

'Marthaaaaaaa,' he hissed, glaring up at her. She tried to pull away but his grip was too strong. He let out a low groan, lips curling ferally back from his teeth.

'It's Ty, sweetheart,' she said softly. 'Martha's gone to—'

'So much *need*,' he said. 'So much…' He paused and stared into her eyes. 'So *bright*.'

And then his eyes snapped shut and he sagged back onto the bed.

'What was that?' asked the doctor, checking the Doctor's readings again.

Ty shook her head. She had no idea. So much of what had happened in the last day or so was beyond her. Here she was – a nurse turned vet – and, just at the moment, she was of use to neither human nor beast.

Suddenly there was a banging and a hammering on the door.

'Who's in there?' shouted someone.

The receptionist rushed to the door, her face pale.

'Who's that?'

'Henig,' came a gruff voice. 'Henig Olssen.'

'Where are the otters?'

'They've gone,' Henig said.

Mariel was already sliding the pole out of the door handles. In rushed Henig with a couple of the other settlers, armed with spades.

'Everyone's gathering in the square – c'mon.'

'I'm not leaving him,' Ty said, glancing at the Doctor.

'Go on,' Lee urged her gently. 'I'll keep an eye on him. He'll be fine now.'

Reluctantly, Ty gave in, and followed Henig and the receptionist out into the crisp night air.

The orange-lit square was filling up with people – crying and shaking people.

'What's happened?' asked Ty, looking around in fear, although she thought she already knew the answer.

It was like the night of the flood, all over again. Ty watched the receptionist run to find her boyfriend and saw her swallowed up by the crowd. There was no one left for Ty to run to.

No one seemed to know exactly what had happened, although one thing was very quickly clear.

Twenty people had completely and utterly vanished.

And Martha Jones was amongst them.

ELEVEN

More than anything, Ty felt she'd let the Doctor down. Back in the bio lab, sitting beside his bed, mopping his forehead and listening to him muttering in his sleep, a tiny, tiny part of her hoped he wouldn't wake up yet. Not until she'd worked out what she was going to say to him.

'Well it's like this…'

'I couldn't stop her…'

'She just ran off…'

No matter how she worded it, she'd let him down. She'd let his best friend run off into the night with nothing more than a high-tech screwdriver.

Reports came back to her about the events of the night before. Doors and walls all around the square were covered with long scratches, and the grass between the buildings bore numerous scuff and drag marks, scattered with clods of turf torn up by frantic, panicking hands. The whole of the Council had disappeared, along with eight others – including Martha. And there were smears of blood on the floor and walls of the hallway to the Council chamber.

Then, as if to hammer the final nail into the coffin of her fears about Martha, someone had found the Doctor's sonic screwdriver at the edge of the square, squashed down into the mud. And no one had seen Col or Candy since earlier the previous day, although Janis said that Candy had come looking for Col round about lunchtime. The only assumption they could make was that they'd been taken by the otters as well.

The flood had cut the settlers' numbers in half; and the otters were whittling down the survivors. At this rate, when the second wave of colonists arrived – if they ever bothered – there would be no one here to greet them. Just a rotting, crumbling settlement and a lot of skeletons.

Ty wanted to cry, but she didn't even have the energy for that. All she could do was sit by the Doctor's bedside and hold his hand.

'Professor Benson…?'

Ty jerked awake suddenly. Candy was standing in the doorway. She was filthy, her face spattered and streaked with mud and crusty green slime. She looked exhausted and, as Ty stood up, she almost collapsed in her arms. Ty manoeuvred her into the chair by the Doctor's bed, and she all but fell into it.

'Where have you *been?*' she asked, her voice equal parts anger and worry.

Candy was shaking, her eyes wide. Ty pulled a blanket from the foot of the Doctor's bed and wrapped it around her before shouting out into the corridor that she wanted a cuppa for her. She crouched down beside the girl and took her hand, holding it tight.

'Where were you? We were worried. The otters—' she began, but Candy was already nodding.

'I know,' she said simply. 'I saw them.'

'You *saw* them?'

Candy nodded, fixing Ty with her eyes.

And then, shakily, she began to tell Ty all about her trip to the *One Small Step*.

'After Col… after he died,' said Candy, 'I tried to drag his body out of the ship. I don't know why. He was dead. There was nothing I could have done. The thing, the tentacle or whatever it was, that had been in his head. It pulled out of the ship. I could hear it slithering and banging down the outside of the ship. When I realised it was pointless, I gave up and started to leave the ship. But there were otters, outside. They looked sort of weird, doped. But I didn't want to risk it, so I made my way back down the ship and managed to get out through one of the rear emergency exits. I hung around though, just to see what they were up to.'

'You should have come straight back,' Ty said.

Candy nodded guiltily.

'I know. But after what had happened to Col, after what I saw… I thought I might be able to find something out.' She gave a half-hearted shrug. 'But I didn't. I watched them moving around the ship for a bit but it was too dark to be able to see much, so I thought I should come back.

'But as I was heading back through the forest, I heard the otters behind me so I hid in a tree and watched them. There were dozens of them – *dozens*! I let them go past and then started following them. They were heading for the city, for here. I knew I'd never catch them up. By the time I got here…' She broke off again, and Ty felt her squeeze her fingers tightly. 'It was too late – they were herding the Councillors back through the forest. Like sheep. Nipping at their legs and feet. Dory Chan was swearing at them like a trooper,' she grinned. 'But they just kept going, forcing them back out into the forest. I hid up a tree. Again.' The poor girl looked as miserable as Ty had ever seen her look. She almost didn't want to ask her next question, but she knew she had to.

'Did you see Martha? We found the Doctor's sonic thing. Martha had taken it with her. No one's seen her since.'

Candy shook her head. 'It was dark, so I *might* have missed her. But I don't think so.'

Ty didn't know whether this was more or less worrying. If Martha *hadn't* been taken by the otters, then *where was she*?

Had Ty but known it, Martha had been almost as confused as her.

She'd stood in the darkness, sonic screwdriver in hand, and watched as a confused and shifting mass of darkness moved across the other side of the square. It took her a few moments to realise what it was: people. A crowd of people. Their movements were odd and jerky, and only when Martha saw the shadows skipping and jumping along the ground did she work out that the crowd of people was being herded by otters.

Martha gritted her teeth and made sure she had a firm grip on the screwdriver. This'd see 'em off.

Only Martha had never got as far as seeing 'em off. Barely had she taken two steps in the direction of the rapidly departing crowd than her feet managed to catch on something. With a loud *ooof!* she went sprawling, full length. Reflexively, her arms shot out to stop herself, and she felt warm fur, slipping and sliding under her hands. Hands that no longer held the Doctor's beloved sonic. In panic, she reached for the ground beneath her, hoping against hope that it would still be there, that she'd feel the comforting solidity of the little device. But all she felt were more otters.

Abandoning her search, fearful of being torn to shreds by their teeth and claws, Martha rolled over onto her side, away from the furry bodies that bounced and jiggled against her. She couldn't tell how many there were – half a dozen? Ten? In seconds she was back on her feet. She raised her hands, defensively – and, to her amazement, the little semicircle of otters backed away from her.

'Keep back,' Martha warned, knowing full well that they wouldn't understand her words, but hoping that, like with wild animals, the tone of her voice would speak volumes.

One of the otters squeaked at her.

At least…

'*What?*' exclaimed Martha.

'Not,' squeaked the otter again, 'hurt.'

'You can *talk?*'

The otters just stared up at her in the near-darkness.

'Not hurt,' the otter repeated, its voice so high-pitched and squeaky that Martha wondered whether she wasn't just hearing something that wasn't there. 'Help us. Help you.'

That clinched it.

'I've got to get back to the Doc—'

'Come,' said a different otter.

'I need to—'

'Come now!'

It was amazing how much urgency the little bear-faced creature could get into its voice. Three or four of the otters moved towards her, their mouths open. Martha could see their gleaming incisors, and suddenly wasn't sure how much trust she could put in 'Not hurt'. Another couple moved in, bumping their noses against her legs, as if urging her on. She flinched, half-expecting to feel teeth sinking softly into her shins.

'OK, OK,' she said, raising her hands and taking a step backwards. 'Point taken.'

With one last look back at Sunday city, Martha let herself be led out into the darkness of the forest.

Ty had stayed with the Doctor for a little while longer. Candy had fallen asleep in the room next door. Half of Ty wanted to play the organiser, the let's-get-things-done-er. The other half just wanted out, away from this hateful planet. It all seemed so *pointless* now. One catastrophe – a catastrophe wrought from the heavens by unthinking nature – was bad enough. They'd managed. They'd coped. But *this*…

Checking the Doctor was sleeping comfortably, Ty wandered miserably across the square to the zoo lab and started to tidy up. After this, she didn't think she'd really want to work with the otters, no matter how things turned out. As she put the cages back in place along the back wall, she wondered whether she ought to go back to nursing. She'd been quite a good nurse, back on Earth, until she'd decided that humans were more than capable of looking after themselves. It was the animal kingdom, suffering at mankind's hands, that needed help more. How the tables had turned, out here amongst the stars. She'd become a vet just a couple of years prior to deciding to come to Sunday – two of the best years of her life. The hardest part about leaving Earth had been finding homes for the menagerie she'd surrounded herself with in those two years – a host of injured and difficult-to-home dogs and cats and guinea pigs, along with two goats, a chinchilla and a cockatoo.

As she rattled the last of the cages into place, there was a noise behind her and she turned sharply to see Candy, standing in the doorway.

'The Doctor's awake,' Candy said simply. 'He's in the bio lab with Orlo – and he wants to see you.'

She saw his spectacled face through the porthole in the door before she entered the darkened bio lab, illuminated by the flickering screens of the video. His eyes made contact with hers as she pushed against the double doors – and something in them drained the fire out of her in an instant.

'Professor Benson,' he said as she entered. 'I owe you an

apology.'

Ty said nothing, letting the doors swing to and fro behind her. Orlo was standing at the end of the table, his arms folded, weight shifted onto one leg. He looked tired and worried.

'What for?'

'Orlo here told me what happened to your people last night. I should have been here to stop it instead of turning myself into a *My First Little Chemistry Set*.'

She glanced at Orlo who gave her a rueful half-smile.

'Well…' began Ty.

She perched herself on the corner of the video table, hoping it was as strong as it looked.

'How are you feeling?' she asked.

'Me? Oh, I'm fine – just fine.' He tipped his head, pulled down one of his eyelids and leaned forwards for her to look. 'That looks fine, doesn't it?' He didn't wait for an answer. 'Good! Only the word is that I turned into something of a green-eyed monster last night.'

'More black than green, really,' Ty said. 'But the monster bit's about right.'

'Sorry I had to put you through all of that, but it was the only way.'

'To find out what the alien proteins were for?'

He nodded.

'Not something I fancy going through again in a hurry, I have to say. But as an intelligence-gathering exercise, it wasn't totally unsuccessful.' He took off his glasses, popped them in his jacket pocket and grinned.

'Those slime-things, the beasties in the nests – I know

what they want.' He paused for dramatic effect. 'Us!' he whispered.

TWELVE

The further she was from the settlement, the more nervous Martha was becoming. She'd lost not only the sonic screwdriver, but also any sense of where she was or where the otters were taking her. After their initial 'conversation', they'd remained largely silent, whispering to each other in tiny squeaks. One or two of them would rush ahead, obviously scouting out the way, and then return. They'd confer with their fellows and then the whole group would move on again. The couple of times that Martha tried to find out where they were all going were met with silence, and she was beginning to wonder whether she'd imagined hearing words in amongst their squeaks.

How come no one had mentioned that they could talk before? She couldn't recall their talking when they'd taken her the first time. Up ahead, a domed black shape showed against the darkness of the forest. Although Martha didn't remember seeing one of the otters' nests from the outside, she knew full well what it was. Her pulse began to quicken and her mouth began to dry as her little furry entourage guided her down a channel-like path into their home.

She had to drop to all fours, feeling the soft mud squelching between her fingers and the wetness soaking through the dressing gown and hospital gown to her knees. And then she was inside. Memories of the last time she'd been in a nest came rushing back and she fought back the rising panic. But as her eyes became acclimatised to the darkness, she realised that this nest was a little different to the other one: the pit at the centre, instead of being filled with water, contained only soil. Otters ran backwards and forwards across it.

'So what now?' Martha said, hunching herself up against the far wall and hooking her arms around her knees. 'Tea would be nice.'

For a moment, she realised that she was sounding like the Doctor. And, in a silly way, it made her feel stronger. If the Doctor could get through the worst of times with a joke and a grin, then why couldn't she? Maybe it was one of those unwritten rules of space and time travel: face it all with a quip or risk going completely barking mad.

The otters that had brought her here lined up around the curve of their nest, linking paws in an incredibly cute way, as if they were about to take a bow at the climax of *Tarka – The Opera*.

'I spose that "take me to your leader" won't help, will it?' Martha suggested – hoping that their leader wouldn't turn out to be one of the slime creatures.

'Leader bad,' said one of them. 'Hurt.'

'Your leader's hurt?'

'Bad leader. Leader hurt. Hurt bad.'

Martha shook her head.

'Just rearranging the words isn't going to help,' she said. 'Is your leader hurt?'

'No leader,' repeated the otter. 'Leader bad. Leader hurt us.'

'Ah!' Martha reckoned it was making a certain kind of sense. 'Right – let me see if I'm getting this right. You don't have a leader, yeah?'

'No leader,' agreed the otter seriously – or as seriously as a squeaking otter could be.

'But *a* leader has hurt you? Something you think of as a leader?'

'Leader hurt us. Bad. Don't want leader. Leader wants us. Leader wants you.'

'And by leader,' Martha ventured, 'you mean those slime-things, don't you? They hurt you, didn't they?'

Martha tried not to think too hard about what the otters' 'leader' had done to her, how it had made her feel – angry, hungry, violent. It had worn off with her as it had worn off with the otters – well, these otters at least. But why *these* otters…? A sudden thought came to her.

'Before,' she said slowly, trying to keep her speech simple. 'Where were you?' She gestured around at them.

'Before?'

'Before you found me. Before you brought me here. After the leader hurt you. Where were you?'

'Square nests,' one of the otters said.

Square nests? What the Dickens were 'square nests'?

But no explanation was forthcoming from the otters.

'So why have you brought me here?'

'Why?' echoed an otter. Martha sighed. Clever the otters might be, but they weren't what she'd call intelligent. Or should it be the other way around?

'Me,' Martha gestured. 'Here.' She paused. 'Why?'

'Help us,' said the otter. 'Help you.'

A bout of squeaking and squeeing ensued and then three of the otters rushed off through a hole in the side of the nest. They returned a few moments later, rolling something the size of a football in front of them. As they pushed it up against Martha's feet, she realised that it was made of a sort of wickerwork, like the roof of the nest. Encouraged by the otters, she picked it up, but it was too dark to see what was inside it – and then, suddenly, the whole thing moved in her hands and she dropped it.

More cautiously this time, she pulled it back towards her and peered through the mesh of reeds. Inside, only just visible, something glistened wetly, shifting about.

'Why would these slime creatures want *us*?' Ty asked the Doctor. 'And what did Col mean about them wanting our intelligence?'

The Doctor tapped his finger against his lip, his eyes narrow.

'It makes a certain kind of sense,' he said eventually. 'What Col said about intelligence, and what I experienced last night.' He pulled out his spectacles, fiddled with them for a few moments, and then put them back. 'What d'you know about SETI?' he asked.

'Another word for a sofa?' Candy suggested.

The Doctor put his spectacles on and peered acidly at her over the top of them.

'Something to do with whales?' Ty ventured. 'Cetaceans?'

He peered again and shook his head.

'What *are* they teaching people in schools these days?' He whipped his glasses off again. 'Come on – we've got work to do,' he said suddenly. He spun around and his fingers dabbed at the video table: the overhead lights came on as the screens went dark. The Doctor raced around Ty to the door.

'Where are you going?' she said, jumping to her feet.

'Where are *we* going, you mean,' replied the Doctor, halfway out of the room.

Ty shook her head and followed, Candy bringing up the rear.

'OK,' Ty called, trying to catch up. 'Where are *we* going?'

'We,' he called back over his shoulder, 'are going to the same place that they've taken the others.'

'Their nests?'

The doors ahead slammed open as the Doctor strode out into the orange daylight.

'Nope,' he shouted. 'The river.'

Ty managed to catch up with him, and Candy jogged to fall into step with him on the other side.

'How d'you know they've gone there?'

He tapped the side of his head.

'That's one of the things the proteins told me.'

'One of them?' Ty asked. 'So they *are* encoding information?'

He pulled a disparaging face.

'As information encoding goes, it's all a bit shoddy – a bit make-do-and-mend. The Urzhers on Mustack would have been able to encode a whole symphony, the complete works of Tschubas and a recipe for chocolate cake into the proteins I injected into myself. But our slimy little friends aren't quite up to the Urzhers' standards.' He waved his fingers in the air dismissively. 'Rather amateur, actually – but I suppose it did its job.'

'Which was...?' asked Ty, clearly starting to get annoyed with his vagueness.

The Doctor rounded the corner and headed into the main square. Ty and Candy ran to keep up.

'They wanted us all fired up, angry, acting on instinct,' he explained. 'It helps to override our intelligence, our free will. My guess is that they're still experimenting, still trying to work out the right proteins, the right RNA strings to pull *our* strings. Oooh !' He glanced at Candy. 'Remind me to use that one again. Where was I? Oh yes,' he plunged on. 'I think they were just testing us – us non-otters, that is. They've had months to practise on them and by now have probably got the hang of pulling *their* strings perfectly. The stuff they injected into Martha – and that I injected into myself – was fairly simple: a few trigger chemicals, a sprinkling of dumb, a bit of angry and just a *soupçon* of greedy. Oh, and some pictures.'

'Pictures? Of what?'

The Doctor had reached the very centre of the square and he stopped dead, spinning around on his heels.

'Swamps, water, otters – just the usual holiday snaps. And a very nice postcard of your old city.'

'The settlement? Why?'

'I think they're curious,' he whispered. 'Very curious.'

'The slime creatures? About the settlement?'

'About us and about what's *in* the settlement. Remember what Col said about them wanting our intelligence? Well intelligence is only useful if directed towards a goal. If it's used for problem-solving. So we need to think along the lines of what problems the slimeys might have. If we can keep one step ahead of them, if we can out-think them, then maybe we've a chance of stopping them. What *is* in the grey building, by the way – the one nearest the bank, the one they were poking around in as I left.'

Ty frowned.

'You mean… the technical services unit?'

'Doesn't sound very exciting, does it,' he murmured, 'The "technical services unit". What's a "technical services unit" when it's at home, then?'

'It's where all the plans for the Sunday City were kept, where all the power and communications were controlled from. Sort of a nerve centre.'

'Ahh…' the Doctor said mysteriously. 'Now that's more like it: a nerve centre. In fact, I think it deserves capitals. A Nerve Centre! And an exclamation mark.'

'Why would the otters want the technic—'

Ty stopped and rolled her eyes as the Doctor raised a finger and an eyebrow.

'Why would the otters want the Nerve Centre?' she said wearily.

'No idea.'

'And what,' said Ty, planting her hands on her hips, 'are we going to fight them with?'

'One of the greatest all-purpose tools that evolution's yet come up with,' the Doctor grinned. He paused, clearly hoping someone would come up with the answer. There was silence.

'I imagine,' he said eventually, 'that the irony of the fact that I'm talking about the human brain will be lost on you both.'

Ty and Candy looked at each other.

'Honestly,' he sighed, 'my wit's wasted on you people, it really is.'

Martha felt the woven ball move slightly in her hands as the thing inside it shifted again. The dim moonlight filtering in through the roof of the otters' nest caught it. It was about the size of a fist but blobby and shapeless. Martha made the instant connection between it and the slime-things.

'It's a *baby* isn't it?' she said in a whisper. 'A baby slime creature!'

The otters squeed and chattered, and little groups of them joined hands as if for mutual support.

'Broken,' said one – the one with the grey smudge on its ear. 'Broken leader.'

Martha didn't understand. Was it ill? Is that how they'd managed to catch it?

'Look,' she said firmly. 'Thanks for the show 'n' tell. But I'm not sure what you want me to do with it.'

'Make broken,' said the otter. 'Make broken.' Others joined in and, within seconds, they were chanting in unison.

Martha sighed, setting the ball down by her knee. She was starting – a bit unfairly – to feel irritated by this half-speech that the otters were giving her.

'You want me to make this more broken?' she asked, gesturing to the shaking ball.

'Leader,' said the one with the smudged ear. 'Make broken.'

Only then did it suddenly hit her: the otters wanted her to do what they couldn't. They wanted her to make the 'leader' – the parent of the thing in the basket – broken.

They wanted her to kill it!

Marj Haddon felt as though she were drowning in slow motion.

Every breath was laboured and painful, like she was breathing treacle. And everything around her was blurred and smeared, as though through a rain-drenched window.

And there was something in her head with her.

She tried to focus – tried to remember how she'd gotten there. Wherever *there* was. All around her, sticking up out of the mud, were buildings – dirty, grubby buildings that looked familiar and yet strange. She struggled to concentrate on them, to understand what they were. But the whispering voices at the back of her head kept distracting her and her awareness kept slipping away. Images of water, sensations of hunger and impatience kept nipping at the edges of her consciousness, like irritating little dogs, eager for her attention. She felt slightly – though not pleasantly – drunk, drifting through this strange world on autopilot.

Again, she tried to work out how she'd gotten from where she'd been before (where *was* that?) to here. A sudden flickering montage of images crashed into her head: things, biting at her legs, scratching her. Screams. People crying. And then the dark of the night and the sounds of stumbling through the forest. And then she was down at the edge of the water, and the water was moving, swirling…

And then…

Nothing.

She was here. Around her, like sleepwalkers, other people drifted like ghosts. Some of them carried things in their hands. Others just shuffled, like clockwork toys that someone had wound up and let go. What were 'clockwork toys'? The thought came and went like a fish in a river, just a shiny sliver of memory, uncatchable, unholdable.

Something in her head told her which way to go.

She moved.

Candy found herself hanging back a little as the three of them reached the rise beyond which lay the start of the old settlement. She could smell the wet and the damp from the flooded river plain ahead, and memories of the evening before, when she'd found Col, came trickling back.

I should have told them, she thought. *I should have said something…*

The little voice had been niggling away inside her ever since she'd returned and told Ty what had happened. She'd been surprised, to be honest, that Ty hadn't pressed the point more firmly: what had Col been doing at the *One Small Step*? Why had he gone out there on his own, without telling anyone?

But Ty's shock at what had happened to him seemed to have swamped all that, and Candy was glad.

The poor man's dead, thought Candy. *Let him rest in peace. What use would it be to tell them?*

'You OK?'

It was the Doctor. He was looking at her strangely, as if he could read her mind. She forced a smile and nodded.

'Just tired,' she said. He nodded as if he understood.

'Maybe you should go back,' he suggested. 'Have a bit of a kip.'

Candy shook her head.

'I'm fine, honestly. What's the plan?'

The Doctor grinned down at her.

'Step one: we find out where they all are. Step two: I use the sonic screwdriver to stun the otters. And step three: we move in and get your people out as quickly as possible.'

'What about the slime creatures?' asked Ty.

'I suspect that they're not going to be much of a problem. So far, they've kept to the water – or pretty close to it. I suspect they're mainly aquatic, and they've used the otters as their hands and eyes and ears – at least until now. So I don't think we have to worry too much about them. Not yet, at any rate. But any sign of them and we leg it – got that?'

Candy and Ty nodded. They dropped to all fours as they reached the crest of the rise. The Doctor glanced back and grinned.

'Let's take a look, shall we?'

On his hands and knees, the Doctor crept to the brow of the hill. Ty glanced nervously at Candy and gave her a tight smile.

'They're there,' the Doctor hissed.

Candy scuttled alongside him.

Down on the mud flats she could see about half a dozen of the settlers. They were drifting in and out of the technical services unit, carrying bits and pieces, plans, wires. They looked like zombies, robots. And amongst them, stationary, like little brown statues, were the otters.

'Why aren't the otters moving?' whispered Candy.

'Probably been given orders just to watch your people. They're the ones that the slimeys are concentrating on.'

'So this control…' It was Ty. 'How does it work? The slimeys put instructions in their heads and then…'

'Then the humans carry them out. They have to be relatively simple: the slimeys' encoding isn't sophisticated enough, yet, to give them very complex tasks. Stuff like "Go there – get this – take it there" I should imagine. And there will be a homing instruction too. The proteins don't last long, so the slimeys need to make sure that the humans go back to them for more instructions before the chemicals break down. If you hadn't tied me down last night, I'd probably have made a break for the water, trying to get back to them. Martha had a similar reaction.'

'Where are the rest of them?'

'They must be busy elsewhere. That's a bit of a bummer, isn't it? Still, can't be helped. If we can rescue these, it's a start.'

He reached down and fished in his pocket for the sonic screwdriver.

'Everybody ready?'

Slowly he stood up, raised the sonic screwdriver and held it out in front of him – and pressed the button.

The tip glowed a fierce blue-white and it began to hum.

And then, with a noise like a rapidly deflating balloon, the light went out.

'What just happened?' asked Candy.

The Doctor shook it and tried again. This time there was nothing – no light, no sound.

He turned sharply to Ty.

'What have you been *doing* with this?'

'What?'

He peered at it closely, shook it – even held it to his ear.

'It's full of *mud*!' he wailed. 'It's dead.'

'It won't be the only thing,' said Ty in a low voice. 'Look…'

Everyone looked over the rise: down below, the otters had seen them and were flowing out from amongst the settlers.

Towards them.

The Doctor sighed. 'Here we go again…'

* * *

'Run!' shouted the Doctor. 'Both of you – get back to the city!'

'No way,' said Candy.

'Candy,' said Ty. 'Go on. I've got two tranq guns in my pocket. Get back to the city and tell everyone what we've seen. Just in case… you know.'

'I'm not going,' Candy said stubbornly. 'You two are no match for the otters.'

'Oh, you'd be surprised,' said the Doctor, his voice steely and determined.

'Especially without your sonic thing.'

'Oh, who needs gadgets? Told you before,' the Doctor said, tapping the side of his head. 'Greatest tool in the galaxy.'

'Someone was being a bit unkind,' Candy couldn't help but joke.

He threw her a sharp look.

'Please, Candy – just go. Tell the settlers what we've found. We'll be back – honest.'

'Why not come with me now, then?'

'Because I want to find out more about what's going on.'

Candy's shoulders fell – she knew that he wouldn't give up until she'd gone.

'Right,' she said eventually. 'Fine. Just… you know.' And before she could stop herself, she gave him a kiss on the cheek. 'Come back, yeah?'

'Yeah,' he smiled. 'Trust me.'

'What, 'cos you're a doctor?'

'No: 'cos I'm *the* Doctor! Now *get moving!*'

Candy glanced back down the slope: the wave of otters

was closer, much closer. With a quick squeeze of Ty's hand, she headed back towards Sunday City.

The otters approached in a broad wave, pausing fifty metres or so away.

'Oh… now *that's* interesting…' The Doctor gestured down the slope.

The otters, like a sea of brown fur, were parting – moving aside to leave a clear path through the centre of them.

'Come into my parlour…' whispered the Doctor. 'Am I the only one to get the feeling we've been set up here?'

Ty glanced to the left and the right and saw that the otters, without being noticed, had executed a perfect pincer movement, slipping behind them. Trapping them.

'I think we're being invited in for a cuppa.'

'We're not going, are we?' said Ty.

'It'd be rude to refuse.'

'You're mad,' said Ty.

'No,' said the Doctor primly. 'Just very well brought up. Come on – if we don't hurry, the tea'll be stewed. And there's nothing worse than stewed tea.'

'Apart from death at the claws of a thousand otters,' she pointed out as the Doctor stepped forward and began to descend the slope.

'Yes,' he said airily over his shoulder. 'There is that.'

Down on the mud flats, the half-dozen humans went about their business silently, like robots. And the otters parted further, funnelling the Doctor and Ty to the edge of the water, which slopped gently up onto the bank and then dropped back, dark and oily, reflecting the growing clouds above them. Ty shuddered.

'If they think I'm going swimming,' she said, 'then they're out of their tiny minds.'

'Oh, I don't think they have tiny minds at all,' the Doctor said. 'Not the slimeys at any rate. In fact I think they have rather large ones. Not their own, granted, but still pretty big. Think of them as time shares.'

He looked down at her and smiled.

'SETI!' Ty cried and snapped her fingers. 'Not settee – SETI! That computer thingy. But that was abandoned *years* ago. My grandpa was really into it. Grandma kept complaining about him leaving the computer on all the time.'

'Knew you'd get there eventually' said the Doctor. 'SETI – the Search for Extra-Terrestrial Intelligence. So, Professor Benson, tell me what you know about it while we wait for the sandwiches and cakes to arrive.'

'This is just so's you can look all smug and clever, isn't it? Go on then: it was some sort of government scheme – American I think – to look for alien signals, radio messages.' She looked at the Doctor. 'Right?'

He just smiled.

'And 'cos it needed loads of computing to analyse the signals, they came up with a sort of time-share plan. People all around the world – ordinary people with computers at home – sort of logged on to this network and let their computer do some of the work for them. I'm right, aren't I?'

'Gold star, Professor,' beamed the Doctor.

'So you're saying that the slimeys are like that – but with *brains?*'

'It fits the evidence. And, as a scientist, you know that that's what science is all about – looking at the evidence and coming up with a theory that fits it. In their natural state, I bet they're pretty stupid – tiny little brains. But when they land on a planet, they find some smart creatures and hijack their brains for a while – get them to do some of the thinking for them. They hive off some thinking, some processing, into – well, say, otters, or people or whatever they can – and then, later, the otters or people go back to the slimeys, upload the results of all that thinking, and the slimeys repeat it again with other otters.'

'Or people,' Ty finished. 'It's horrible.'

'It's very effective, though.'

Ty was appalled at the Doctor's attitude.

'The slimeys use the resources of the planets they infect – no need to carry around whopping great brains of their own. And it means they begin with a head start, as it were. Who better than the natives to know how the local environment works, where stuff is, what the weather's like, where the best coffee shop is. Instinct becomes intelligence – just like that! Straight to Mayfair, collect two hundred pounds. *Brilliant!*'

But the expression on his face changed as the waters before them began to swirl and churn. Ty took a step back – only to discover that the otters had enclosed them, trapping them against the shore.

'You know what you said earlier,' Ty whispered. 'About the slimeys being aquatic, and how we'd be safe if we stayed away from the water…'

Suddenly, the surface of the river was broken with a huge, foamy splash.

A figure rose up from the water, drenching them all. Ty steeled herself for one of the tendrils that had attacked Martha in the nest.

But the thing that came towards them was the last thing she had expected to see.

It was Pallister.

THIRTEEN

Pallister stared at them with dead, black eyes, sparkling wetly like the carapaces of monstrous insects. His upright body swung limply, like a corpse, as it floated towards them across the water. Its feet dragged the surface, and they could see the huge tendril that supported him from behind. It split into three smaller ones, moistly green, piercing his skull at the back and the sides, like fingers stuck into a ten-pin bowling ball. They pulsed and throbbed, as if they were pumping fluids in and out of the man's brain. Ty shuddered, realising that this must have been how Col had died.

'You,' said Pallister, his voice bubbling and dribbling from his mouth like oil, 'will be me.'

'Is that right?' said the Doctor archly, folding his arms. 'Well excuse me if I decline your very kind offer. I rather enjoy being *me*, actually.'

Pallister – or the thing that controlled him – seemed to consider the Doctor's words for a moment. Water dripped from the man's clothes into the river, sending little ripples out across its surface.

'It's processing,' the Doctor whispered to Ty out of the corner of his mouth. 'The thing that's operating poor old Pallister is using his brain to translate. Much quicker than time-sharing the otters' brains, I imagine.'

'Why?' came the reply, after what seemed like forever.

'Why?' said the Doctor indignantly. '*Why*? Why d'you think? I was born me, I've lived my life – well, most of it – as me, and I'd rather like to carry on being me. That's the way I am.'

Pallister's body twitched as one of the creature's tendrils jerked.

'To work as one,' it said slowly, 'is better. Unity is better than diversity.'

'Says who?'

'Pallister thinks that. It is in accord with me.'

The Doctor blew a raspberry.

'I wouldn't take much notice of poor old Pallister. Bit up himself if you ask me. And if you had better access to his brain, you'd see that there's a big difference between "unity" and "obsessive single-mindedness".' He paused and leaned forwards slightly. 'But you can't, can you? I mean, you weren't exactly at the front of the queue when evolution handed out brains, were you?'

Pallister blinked slowly with a cold superiority. He said nothing.

'See!' cried the Doctor smugly. 'You haven't a clue what I'm talking about! All your intelligence *is* just time-shares, isn't it?' The Doctor turned to Ty with a grin. 'What did I tell you? This thing's just renting rooms in other people's heads.'

'Well,' Ty muttered dourly, 'the landlord isn't going to be too pleased about what his new tenant's done to the property.' She looked at Pallister, his skin puffed and bloated, the holes in his head where the creature's tentacles fed in.

'Interesting evolutionary tactic,' the Doctor mused, peering at Pallister again. 'Just squat in the brains of the creatures on whatever planet you find yourself on. Shame that I'm here to hand out an eviction notice to you. You've got exactly ten minutes to vacate the property before I send the bailiffs in.'

Pallister said nothing – and Ty suspected that the creature controlling him hadn't understood a word of it.

'What the Doctor means,' she added loudly, 'is *Get your miserable ass out of there!*'

The Doctor looked at her, a hurt expression on his face.

'That's what I said!'

'Like you said,' Ty whispered, 'it's not the brightest of things.'

'No,' he agreed, 'but it's bright enough to trick us into coming here, I think. What's that all about then?' He was addressing Pallister. 'I mean, you obviously need these people to do some dirty work for you. But you'd programmed the otters to bring us to you before we even arrived, otherwise they'd have torn us to pieces by now. Why?'

'To assess you,' Pallister said. 'He and the others knew you would come to me. Pallister thinks that you are intelligent, that you might serve my purpose.'

'What d'you hope to gain from using Pallister, anyway?' Ty asked the crumbling husk hanging before them.

'Yes,' agreed the Doctor. 'What's the point of this ridiculous puppet show? Not going to bring on a crocodile with a string of sausages, are you?'

'Sausages?' said Ty.

'Never seen a Punch and Judy show?' sighed the Doctor.

'Normal communication with you is inefficient,' Pallister intoned, ignoring the Doctor's ramblings.

'Well it would be,' agreed the Doctor. 'We're not well equipped for your particular brand of chemical chat.'

'This mode will facilitate the extraction of information useful to reproduction.'

The Doctor pulled a face.

'You do realise that you've put images in my head that even industrial-strength mind bleach isn't going to erase, don't you?' he said. 'How many of you are there, then? How many of you came down with that meteorite?'

'I am one.'

'Just the one? Well, you *have* been putting yourself about a bit. You must be *huge* then!' He stopped. 'And what d'you mean, "useful to reproduction"? What has Pallister got to do with it? And do I really want to hear the answer…?'

Ty noted the change in tone in his voice, from bright and cheery to thoughtful and concerned. It didn't sound good.

'The information Pallister contains will facilitate my reproduction. And Pallister thinks you can add to that information.'

The Doctor rolled his eyes.

'We *are* going to be here all day. What information could Pallister possibly have that could help you spawn or bud or whatever it is you do?'

There was another agonising pause whilst the swamp thing processed the Doctor's words through Pallister's brain. The man's eyes were still coal-black and emotionless, but Ty thought she saw just a twitch of his mouth. One arm shuddered, sending more drips of water into the river below.

'It believes that I should not tell you,' came Pallister's voice after a few moments.

'It?' the Doctor shouted. '*It? It* is a human being; *it* is a man called Pallister. *He* might have been a bit rough around the edges, but at least he had the interests of the people here at heart. Sort of,' the Doctor finished a little lamely.

'And I have my interests,' replied Pallister. 'Reproduction is the purpose of life.'

'Oh tosh!' snapped the Doctor. 'It might be quite useful but it's not the be-all and end-all, you know. What about exploring? What about music and dancing and climbing mountains? What about adventure and love and laughing? What about jigsaws, eh?' He jabbed a finger in Pallister's direction. '*That's* what the purpose of life is – living.'

'Reproduction is my purpose.'

The Doctor shook his head and threw up his hands theatrically.

'Well there you go, then.' He turned to Ty. 'I told you this thing had no brain – and now we know it's got no heart or soul either. And what exactly does your reproduction involve, then, eh?' he said to Pallister. 'Spores? Buds? Dozens of little slime babies popping out of your tentacles?' He paused and pulled a face. 'Ew, slime babies.' He gave a theatrical little shudder. 'I'll never eat a jelly baby again.'

'Pallister thinks you are asking in order to use the information against me.'

'Oh does he? I'm not sure you can trust the word of a man with a couple of pounds of slime squidged into his head. Plays havoc with the synapses, believe me.'

'Doctor,' said Ty suddenly. Extruding itself from the main tendril supporting Pallister's body was another, thinner one. Glassy and glistening, like the one that had attacked Martha in the nest, it was heading towards the Doctor.

'Time for bed,' whispered the Doctor as it wove sinuously through the air.

'You will be me,' intoned Pallister soullessly.

'Not today, thank you!' shouted the Doctor – and reached down to grab one of the tranq guns from Ty's hand.

'Will that penetrate it? Remember how tough the one that attacked Martha was!'

'Oh,' he said casually, 'it's not slimey I'm aiming for!'

The Doctor stretched out his arm and there was a soft *pht* as the dart embedded itself in the remains of Pallister's chest.

Seconds later, the barely living body twitched as if it were being electrocuted, and the tendrils supporting it jerked back. The one lancing through the air, heading for the Doctor, began waving and thrashing about aimlessly.

'I think I might have given it a bit of a headache,' the

Doctor noted drily.

Around them, the otters were motionless. The zombified settlers continued to drift in and out of the grey building as if nothing were happening.

Suddenly, Pallister's body shuddered, like a dog shaking itself dry. Then, still suspended by the pulsing green ropes boring into its head, it plunged back into the water.

'Wait!' called the Doctor, his tone mock-offended. 'Where are you going? You were going to tell me about how babies are made and everything! You were going to give us tea and cake!'

But it was too late. Without another word, Pallister vanished beneath the black waters, leaving just a trail of tiny bubbles.

'Oh!' said the Doctor snappily. 'How very rude!'

'What did he mean?' asked Ty. 'About the reproduction.'

'I'm not sure,' replied the Doctor. 'But you have to admit – it didn't sound good, did it? I mean, one of those things is bad enough. But if it's planning on reproducing…' He rubbed the back of his neck and stared at the now-placid surface of the water.

Ty looked at the otters, standing along the bank. Their faces were blank, but she could feel their eyes boring into them.

'Now what?' she said.

'Well,' said the Doctor, ruffling his hair. 'My guess is that the otters are still following their instructions to guide us down to the water and not let us retreat. And if we try to move, I suspect that they'll have a pretty good go at tearing us limb from limb.'

He scratched his chin.

'What we could really do with now is a miracle.'

'A miracle?' scoffed Ty, watching the otters as they stood, teeth bared, all around them.

'Yes,' said the Doctor firmly. 'A miracle. A miracle a bit like *that* one.'

He was staring over Ty's shoulder. She turned to see what he was looking at.

Over the crest of the hill, whooping and shouting fit to scare cattle, was Martha Jones – accompanied by the dirtiest dozen of otters Ty had ever seen – all screeching and squealing and leaping up and down as they came.

'You have *got* to be kidding,' Ty gasped.

Martha had been no less amazed herself, as she stood at the brow of the hill, accompanied by the otters, and watched the dangling figure of a man, supported by a whopping great tentacle, crash back into the water.

She'd arrived just in time to see the end of what looked like a showdown between the 'man' and the Doctor and Ty, down at the edge of the water. The Doctor had raised his arm and fired what looked like a tiny gun at the puppet-man. Seconds later, it had all been over. Well, apart from the fact that Ty and the Doctor were now surrounded by dozens of otters, hemming them in, trapping them on the mud.

'Do something!' Martha urged her furry friends. 'Help them!'

An outbreak of squeaking broke out amongst the otters

at her feet, interspersed with odd words: 'Call them!', 'Help them!', 'Talk! Talk!'

'Will they understand you?' she asked the otters.

'They?' the one with the smudged ear repeated whilst his (her? Martha hadn't thought to check what sex he was – and, to be quite honest, couldn't tell even now) fellows squeaked and chattered.

Martha pointed to the otters surrounding the Doctor and Ty.

'Can you talk to them? You – talk? To them?' She jabbed her hands back and forth frantically, like an inadequately prepared foreign tourist.

But the smudgey-eared one stared at her. 'Talk, no,' he squeaked. Martha's shoulders fell. 'Shout, yes!' he added.

'Shout?'

'Yes – can shout. Might scare.'

'Nice one!' cried Martha, reaching down to stroke his head – but he pulled back, a look of alarm on his little bear-face. 'Might scare is good! Definitely might-scare! Shout,' she added. 'Oh yes!'

And so, like some sort of wild woman, shrieking and wailing as she went, Martha led her band of equally wild otters over the hill and down the slope towards the Doctor and Ty.

Analysing it later, the Doctor coolly said that he wasn't really surprised that the zombie otters took notice of them. Yeah, Doctor. Right. The slime-thing's chemical control was a blunt instrument, not capable of subtle programming: 'Bring humans! Guard humans! Don't let humans go!' That sort of thing. It hadn't counted on other *otters* jumping in to start issuing commands, never mind commands that conflicted with its own.

As the guard-otters saw – and, more importantly, heard – Martha's little strike-force hurtling down the slope, they began to move, glancing at each other, quivering in their little furry boots, giving every impression of being confused.

In amongst all the squeaks and cries her otters bellowed, Martha heard the odd word: 'Run!' and 'Hide!' and 'Water-teeth coming!' What 'water-teeth' were, Martha could only imagine – probably some predator that hid in the swamps and of which the otters were mortally afraid. It was this latter that seemed to have the greatest effect. For within seconds, as Martha's team reached the others, the slime-thing's conditioning finally broke. And in a mad, panicky flurry, the zombie otters fled, scattering out across the slope in a storm of fur and squeals.

'General Martha Jones of the Seventh Cavalry,' said Martha, saluting smartly, 'to the rescue – sir!'

'General Jones!' beamed the Doctor, returning the salute. 'I'm going to be recommending you for a commendation. Come here!'

And he swept her up in a huge hug, lifting her feet clear off the ground.

'Now,' he said, dropping her back on her feet with a jolt and looking around at the sleepwalking settlers. 'Let's see if we can't wake these sleeping beauties up.'

The sun had vanished behind the clouds and the rain had

begun to fall again as the strange little band reached Sunday City.

Waking the hypnotised settlers had been surprisingly easy without the otters there to guard them. The Doctor went to each one in turn, whispered in their ears and then clicked his fingers in front of them. One by one, they'd come out of their chemically induced trance, eyes wide and apparently stunned to find themselves standing ankle-deep in mud on the edge of the old city.

The Doctor pointed them in the direction of Martha and Ty, standing at the brow of the hill and, like acquiescent children, they'd trooped up there to join them.

The journey back had been a sombre affair: Martha and Ty had wanted to talk to the settlers, find out what had happened, what they'd thought they were supposed to be doing. But the Doctor had cautioned against hassling them too much: they'd been through a lot, and he thought they needed to get back to familiar surroundings before the interrogation started.

So they passed the trip with Ty and the Doctor explaining to Martha exactly what they'd encountered down at the water's edge; Martha, likewise, explained all about her little trip to the otters' nest. She'd recovered the basket with the baby slimey-thing in, that she'd left at the brow of the hill. Of the otters – both friendly and unfriendly, there was no sign. Martha hoped that their brave actions hadn't put any of them in danger, but the Doctor reassured her that the brainwashed otters were unlikely to have been any threat to the others.

'I think we have you to thank for them,' the Doctor said to Ty.

'The one with the smudge on its ear?' Ty said. 'Thought I recognised him.'

'What?' said Martha, still trying to work out whether she should be indignant that, somehow, Ty was getting the credit for her perfectly organised and executed rescue.

'Your little *A-Team*,' the Doctor explained, turning the spherical basket over in his hands and making silly cooing noises into it. 'They were Ty's otters – the ones she'd had in the zoo lab.'

'How d'you know?' Martha asked.

'Ty here recognised the one with the smudge and the rest was just obvious, wasn't it Ty?'

Martha felt her teeth grit, all of their own accord, but managed an interested 'Really?'-type smile.

'Well, old slimey-boy seems to have most of the otters hereabouts under its slippery little thumb: it's only the ones that had been in the zoo lab, with the control chemicals decaying, that haven't. Obviously, they had enough intelligence to keep well away from the water and the slime-thing once the intelligence-suppressing chemicals wore off. And when the controlled ones went on their kidnapping rampage here, your friends took the opportunity to let themselves out of their cages and decided that *we* were their best chance to help get rid of slimey.'

The other settlers rushed out to greet them, but there was a sense of defeat in the air at the fact that they hadn't managed to rescue all of the kidnapped humans. No one seemed concerned about Pallister, and Martha realised that she had no idea whether he had any family or friends. It left her feeling a bit cold, a bit detached.

'You OK?'

It was the Doctor, a hand squeezing her shoulder.

'Yeah,' she said as brightly as she could. 'Yeah, I'm fine.'

'You did good, you know,' he said, as Ty vanished into the crowd of settlers, telling them all about what had happened and escorting the rescued ones away.

'Thanks,' said Martha, smiling tightly, watching Ty go.

'In a minute,' the Doctor said, tossing the wicker ball into the air over his shoulder as he strode off towards the zoo lab, 'I think it's time to have a good look at all creatures, erm, small.'

Martha caught it perfectly, watching his back as he went.

'Good catch!' he called out.

'Yeah,' said Martha drily. 'It's what I'm good at.'

'But first, we have a few people to chat to.'

FOURTEEN

The rescued settlers had been gathered in the hospital, where Sam Hashmi and his staff were checking them over, giving them food and drink and generally making sure they were OK. The Doctor whirled in, Martha at his heels, and surveyed the scene.

'Gently does it, I think, Doctor Jones,' he said quietly. 'They probably won't have much conscious memory of what they were doing or how they got there, so let's tread softly. Relax them, try to get them to go back, in their heads, to earlier on.'

Martha suppressed a little shudder, remembering what had happened to her when her memory had been jolted too suddenly. From what she'd heard, she'd been quite a handful. And that was just *one* of her. The thought of half a dozen snarling, snapping people didn't exactly fill her with joy.

The Doctor moved to cover one side of the room; Martha picked out a woman – a kindly, motherly looking woman with silvery-white hair and pale skin. She was perched on the edge of a bed, sipping at a mug of tea.

'Hi,' she said, sitting down beside her. 'I'm Martha. How're you?'

The woman – whose name, Martha discovered, was Marj – smiled tightly, gripping the mug as if it were the only solid, stable thing in her world.

'Fine,' she said. 'Just fine.'

'Just wanted to see if there was anything you remembered – you know, about *before*.'

Marj stared away into the distance.

'Marj?'

'It was like…' Marj stumbled for words. 'Like being in someone else's head. Looking out through their eyes.' She turned to Martha. 'Does that make sense?'

'You've no idea,' Martha replied. 'It happened to me too. Horrible, isn't it?'

'It's the loss of control,' Marj continued, now staring down at the mug that she held firmly on her lap. 'The feeling of being violated, of everything that's *you* just being pushed aside for that… that…' She couldn't finish the sentence.

Abruptly, the mug dropped from her fingers and crashed to the floor, tea splashing across the wooden floor like a wave breaking on a shore. Martha's mouth went dry and, for just a moment, an image of cool, clear water sprang into her head.

Suddenly the Doctor was there in front of her, squatting down, his eyes level with hers.

'I don't know if I can do this,' she whispered.

'Course you can, Doctor Jones,' he said. 'Just remember – the chemicals are gone from you. That thing has no power over you any more.'

'But what about us?' It was Marj, her voice clipped and trembling. 'What about me?'

'That's why Martha needs to speak to you now,' said the Doctor gently. 'Before the chemicals in you vanish completely. You'll be fine, trust me. But we need to find out what you were being made to do. You do understand, don't you?'

Marj nodded uncertainly.

'Good. Let me get you some more tea, and you have a chat with Martha. There's still a dozen settlers out there, and anything you can tell us might help to get them back.'

There was another nod from Marj, and she tried to smile.

'OK, said Martha. 'Let's start at the beginning, shall we…?'

'Useless!' said Martha. 'Absolutely useless!'

'Oh come on! You're not—'

The Doctor stopped when he saw the expression on Martha's face. She wasn't in the mood for his usual brand of jokiness. He sighed and plonked himself on the bed next to her.

'Sadly,' he said, 'I'm inclined to agree with you. There's just not enough to go on – not without poking deeply enough to trigger psychotic episodes like you suffered. I'd try a bit of hypnosis if I didn't think it'd be too intrusive.'

Martha nodded. 'It's like most of them didn't even know what the objects were that they'd been told to fetch. They're like dogs, trained to fetch a newspaper without even knowing what a newspaper *is*.'

'And their memories are fading quickly,' the Doctor sighed. 'Human brain chemistry's obviously more resilient than the otters'. And let's face it, if *I* wasn't able to get anything out of what happened to me, what chance have these poor people?'

Suddenly, Martha's hand flew to her mouth. 'Hang on!' she whispered. 'You said that hypnosis would be too intrusive, yeah?'

The Doctor looked at her thoughtfully. 'Go on…'

Martha narrowed her eyes. 'Tell me I'm wrong, that I haven't grasped how the psychic paper works, but couldn't you—'

'Yes!' The Doctor leaped up and almost punched the air. Martha almost fell over. 'Why didn't I think of that? Martha Jones, you just keep getting better and better!'

'Does that mean I get TARDIS driving lessons?'

'Don't push it,' he said, grinning. 'But I might show you how to change the spare wheel. C'mon!'

'Just take a few deep breaths,' said the Doctor to Marj. 'Let yourself relax… that's it… Now: look at this piece of paper. Try to think about what you were doing, what you were carrying, back there at the settlement. Tell me what you see.'

Martha watched Marj closely, saw the puzzlement

on her face – puzzlement that was suddenly replaced by incredulity.

'How…' she began. 'That's… that's…' She tipped her head slightly, as if the angle of whatever she was seeing was wrong. 'That's… it looks like some sort of circuit, doesn't it? An electronic circuit.' She looked up at the Doctor and Martha. 'Is that right?'

The Doctor whipped the psychic paper back into his pocket and grinned.

'Oh yes, Marj. That's *so* right. Now, you have a nice sleep. You'll feel much better when you wake up. *Believe me.*'

Marj smiled gently, nodded, and lay back on the bed. Within seconds, she was asleep.

'Wow!' Even Martha was impressed. 'Does that help, though?'

'Oh yes – and I've only just started. Care to accompany me on my rounds?'

It took less than half an hour. Of the six settlers they'd brought back, only one was unable to remember anything. The others, to varying degrees, responded well to the psychic paper, letting it gently draw out the buried memories of what the slime creature had commanded of them, what they'd been told to fetch, where they'd been told to take it. To Martha, none of the individual bits and pieces meant much, but the Doctor was getting more and more excited.

When the last of the rescuees was sleeping soundly, he let out a quietly triumphant '*Yes!*'

'And?'

'Slimey-boy out there is making something – *building* something.'

'Like what?'

'Something big and chunky. A bit like me,' he said, 'only with added electronics.'

'They're building a fruit machine?' grinned Martha.

'Oh, please,' the Doctor said, his mouth downcast. 'One of those dance-step machines at the very least. Still, I'll let it all stew in the Doctor-o-tronic for a while.' He tapped his head. 'We'll have a look at baby slimey. Maybe that'll supply the missing bits.'

The zoo lab was deserted: Ty had left a note pinned to the cage in which she'd placed the wicker sphere containing the baby slimey: *Gone to find Candy – thought you'd like the honour of checking out Junior. Love, Ty. xx*

'So,' said Martha as the Doctor popped his glasses on and set about cutting through the otters' handiwork to the thing that flopped inside. 'This Ty. What's she like, then?'

He didn't look up.

'Ty? Oh, she's nice.'

'Oh,' said Martha. 'How old is she?'

'Mmm, dunno really. Best ask her.' He pulled a face as he snipped through more of the twigs and grass, opening up a circular hole at the top. 'Why?'

'Just wondering, really. Seems quite a mother-figure, doesn't she?'

'Does she?'

'Older than my mum, I reckon.'

'Yeah?' The Doctor turned the ball in his hands, jiggling it to shake the thing inside out into a plastic bowl.

'At least,' Martha said, watching his face.

'Gotcha!' he cried as the thing plopped out. He tossed the ball away into a corner.

'I s'pose it's all relative, though, isn't it?' Martha mused.

The Doctor picked up a couple of long pairs of tweezers and began pulling and tugging at the thing in the dish. It reminded Martha of a greeny-black cow's tongue – about six inches long and four across, one end rounded, the other raggedly flat, as though it had been cut.

'Is it?'

'I mean, with you being 900-and-odd. Anyone less than, ooh, 200 must seem much the same.'

'Yeah,' said the Doctor. 'Probably.'

Suddenly, he looked up at her and took his glasses off. 'Martha,' he said, his tone suddenly very different.

'Yeah?'

'You mentioned babies,' he said.

Whoah! thought Martha, suddenly thrown. *Where had* this *come from?*

'Babies?'

He nodded.

'Did I?'

'Well…,' he sucked in his cheeks and looked down at the thing slowly writhing in the dish. 'Baby. Singular.'

'What?'

'This little beauty. You said it was a baby slimey.'

She pulled a stupid face. She couldn't keep up. '*What?*'

'This,' he said, holding it up with a pair of tweezers where it twirled and twisted like the biggest slug Martha had ever seen. 'You said it was a baby.'

'Yeah,' she said, and couldn't have sounded less interested if it had been something he'd pulled out from under a car bonnet.

'Well you were wrong – and right.' He put it back in the dish. 'Look at that flat edge: this has been *cut*. Cut from the tip of one of the big slimey's tentacles. Probably poked itself into your chums' nest and they managed to slice it off. There are fragments of stone in the cut end: language *and* tool-making, eh? Your furry friends are looking cleverer by the minute.

'And the "right" bit?'

'Well…' He popped his glasses back in his pocket and leaned back in his chair, hands clasped behind his head. 'It's a baby too – given the right environment and food, this little chap could grow up just like his daddy. Or mummy. Which is a bit disturbing, considering what Pallister was talking about.'

'That's how slimey reproduces, then? Chop off a bit of him and it grows into a new one?'

'Looks like it. Give me another half hour with him and I'll know for sure.' He paused and looked up expectantly. 'And although it'd be dreadfully sexist of me to suggest it, a cuppa wouldn't half go down well right about now.'

Martha raised an eyebrow at him. 'I'll let you off, just this once. One lump or two?'

* * *

Martha ran – almost literally – into Ty as she was fetching the Doctor his tea. They almost collided on the steps of the zoo lab. Ty looked flustered – something that Martha would never have imagined Ty could look.

'I can't find her,' she said.

'Who?'

'Candy. No one's seen her.'

'But she came back here.'

Ty shook her head. 'I don't think she did: she left us, but there's been no sign of her at all.'

'She must be *somewhere*. Why wouldn't she have come straight back here…?' Even as she asked the question, Martha knew the answer. Well, one possible answer. Two, actually. 'Maybe she decided to see if she could find the other settlers,' she suggested, wrapping her hands around the cooling mug.

'And maybe she got caught,' Ty supplied the second possibility. 'Why didn't she just do what the Doctor said and come back here?'

Martha raised an eyebrow. 'Well,' she said wryly, 'sometimes people don't. Do what the Doctor says, I mean.'

'He's usually right, though.'

'Usually,' Martha agreed. 'But not always. He does tend to get a bit bossy sometimes – makes people do the opposite, you know, just to show they've got a bit of independence.'

Listen to me! thought Martha. *Some friend I am, slagging him off behind his back!*

'Sounds like you're speaking from personal experience,' Ty said with a smile.

Martha tried to brush it off. 'Nah,' she said. 'He's not like that with me.'

'Yeah?'

Martha nodded confidently. 'Wouldn't dare.'

Ty laughed out loud. 'I can believe that, honey. How long you two been together?'

'Together?' Martha suddenly felt herself blush. 'Oh, it's not like that.'

'No? What is it like, then? You his youthful sidekick, like in the movies?'

It was Martha's turn to laugh. 'Something like that: Smith and Jones, we are. Like that old cowboy thing – I think. Unless it's the comedy show…'

'Oh, I think I've seen that. The cowboy one, I mean. And you're… which one?'

Martha pushed open the door to the zoo lab, tea slopping from the mug. 'I'm the pretty one,' she said. 'And don't let him tell you otherwise.'

'What Pallister said,' Ty asked. 'What that *thing* said – about reproduction? What did it mean?'

A couple of dozen Sundayans, along with the Doctor, Martha and Ty, had gathered in the Council chamber around a roaring fire. Ty had found some new, clean clothes for Martha – a weird, shapeless orange kaftan thing that Martha was too polite to decline. She sat alongside the Doctor, picking half-heartedly at a plate of cheese and fruit and fried eggs that she'd been given.

'That's what I've been wondering too,' he replied.

He perched himself on the corner of the council table and pulled an assortment of thoughtful faces. Ty brought around a tray of coffee and more of the 'sap tea' – which wasn't nearly as bad as it sounded.

'What do we know about this thing, then?' the Doctor continued. 'There's just the one of it, it's absolutely *massive*, and it's gobbling up everything around it to make itself even massiver. Makes sense that it lives in water, really – the buoyancy will help support its body, a bit like whales. And it'll have all the seafood it needs. And judging by the bit that Martha here brought back, it reproduces by binary fission, splitting off bits of itself. I had a good poke at it: distributed nervous system, no single brain, no particularly specialised organs. Chop it into a million, billion pieces and before you know it, you've got a million billion new ones.' He pulled a thoughtful face. 'Would explain a lot about its intelligence too – or relative lack of. With a nervous system and "brain" spread throughout its enormous body, it's a fairly slow thinker. There's a limit to how fast nerve impulses can travel through its tissue. One reason why humans are so smart: small, very dense brains, fast communication between different parts of them. This thing,' he grimaced, 'was hiding at the bottom of the sea when Mother Nature handed out smarts. Unfortunately for us and the otters, it's turned a disadvantage into a whopping great *ad*vantage. Instead of trying to do its own thinking, it gets other, brighter species to do it for it. And in the process benefits from those other species' knowledge of the environment that it finds itself in.'

'And it's taken our people,' grunted Henig, sprawled in a wooden chair near the fire.

Martha saw the flicker of acknowledgment in the Doctor's eyes. He'd tried to get all the kidnapped settlers back, but had failed. And the Doctor didn't do failure well.

'It can grow as big as it needs, and has no predators here on Sunday. And judging by its rate of cell division, it's not planning on dying of old age any time soon so it doesn't need children competing for resources.' He shook his head and fixed Henig with a look. 'So there's really only one reproductive strategy that makes sense. That picture you drew, Martha, when we brought you back from the otters' nest: that single great blob enveloping the planet. Well if it's got *this* planet sewn up all by itself, what would be the purpose of reproducing, eh?' He looked round the room like a schoolteacher waiting for the right answer to an algebra question.

'To spread to other planets?' ventured Martha.

'First-class honours!' he grinned. 'To spread to other planets. After all, I think we can be fairly sure that it arrived on – or in – the meteorite that caused the flood.'

'OK,' said Martha thoughtfully, settling back into a chair and putting her fingers together like some sort of evil genius. 'But it can't exactly conjure itself another meteorite out of nowhere to hitch a ride on; it can't repair the settlers' ship; and it doesn't have the brains to make itself a great big space catapult to shoot its little babies into outer space with.' Suddenly, Martha's mouth dropped open. 'Unless *that's* what it was getting the settlers to build – you know, what we learned from them with the psychic paper!'

The Doctor shook his head. 'Too small. Much too small. And too simple, judging by how few parts were involved.'

'Maybe it naturally has the ability to fire bits of itself out there,' Ty suggested. 'There are a few plant species that do that, you know. The stage trees, for example, and the Krynoids, and the comet flowers on Besseme. Maybe this thing does too.'

'It's possible,' considered the Doctor. 'But remember what it said about Pallister – that the information he contained "would facilitate its reproduction". I don't imagine Pallister was a secret expert on building a giant space catapult—' He stopped suddenly. 'What *was* Pallister's speciality?'

Henig pulled a gruff face.

'He was a jumped-up little nobody, that's what was so special about him. That thing sticking its fingers in his head was the most special thing that happened to him in his life.'

There was a murmur of discontent from the assembled settlers. Whatever anyone had thought of Pallister whilst he was alive, they didn't like hearing ill spoken of him now.

'What?' said Henig, rounding on them. 'Don't pretend that you lot didn't think the same? He weaselled his way to the head of the Council, we all know that. And not one of us had the guts to stand up to him and put him in his place.' He scowled. 'If you ask me, that thing and him were made for each other – no wonder it chose *him*.'

'Yes,' said the Doctor. 'That's what I was getting at: *why* did it choose him?' He scratched the back of his head. 'It might just be that it saw some sort of kindred spirit in

Pallister, I suppose, or that it recognised him as your leader and thought that he'd make the best figurehead. So what *did* he do – before he became head of your Council?'

'He was a technician,' said Henig.

'What kind of a technician? Where did he work?'

Henig's eyes suddenly went wide. Ty was a step ahead of him already. 'He worked in the power station and helped set up the refinery,' she said. 'The ore refinery.'

The Doctor's shoulders fell. 'Don't tell me,' he said heavily. '*Uranium* ore. For that beautiful uranium-powered spaceship of yours.'

Ty nodded, her mouth suddenly dry.

'And a man that knows all about how to refine and use uranium,' said the Doctor slowly, 'is now dangling from the end of that creature's tentacles. If we thought things were bad before, I have a terrible feeling that they're only going to get worse. Much, much worse.'

'Why?' barked Henig, frowning. 'The ship needs more than power to get it off the ground – it needs a miracle. It needs parts and repairs and—'

'You're thinking like a human,' the Doctor interrupted, his face becoming grimmer by the second. 'If *you lot* wanted to leave Sunday, you'd need a ship. Slimey out there, on the other hand, doesn't. And you can do a lot more with refined uranium than just power a spaceship…'

He caught Martha's eye. It took her a few moments to catch up – and even then, she didn't quite believe it. 'You have *so* got to be kidding,' she said eventually. 'That thing is going to build a *bomb*?'

The Doctor's gaze didn't waver.

Martha went on, hardly believing the words she was saying. 'It's going to use Pallister's knowledge to build an atomic bomb – and *blow* itself into space? *That's* what the settlers were making?'

Ty shook her head. 'I might only be a zoologist, but even I know that setting off a nuclear bomb right under your ass isn't just going to fling you to your next home.'

The Doctor gave a shrug. 'It's survived the journey to Sunday well enough, though – floating between the stars as a little blob on that asteroid. There's a lot of very hard radiation out there, extremes of temperature.' He drummed his fingers against his bottom lip. 'In fact,' he said, in that tone of voice that made Martha's spirits sink, 'that would make perfect sense. But I don't think we need to worry about that. After all,' he grinned, 'to make a plan like that actually work, it'd need a shaft down into the planet – ooh, a few hundred metres deep, at least. And where's it going to find one of those around here…?'

Martha looked round the room. An awkward hush had fallen. It couldn't have been more obvious, she thought, than if someone had pulled out a great big photo of a hole in the ground, with all the Sundayans standing around it, pointing, holding up a sign saying 'Great big hole in the ground'.

'Oh great,' said the Doctor, his shoulders sinking. 'Just *great!*'

FIFTEEN

Candy knew she ought to feel guilty for coming back here on her own, ignoring the Doctor's instructions. But, really, she didn't. She'd never been good at taking orders, even from someone as likeable as the Doctor. And besides, she knew that his 'Tell the settlement!' had just been an excuse to get her out of danger. What could she have told them that they didn't already know, or couldn't have guessed?

No, it made more sense for her to find the rest of the kidnapped Sundayans. Even if she couldn't actually rescue them, she could at least let everyone else know exactly where they were. Brains might not have been Candy's forte, but getting stuck in certainly was.

So she started off back to the city, and then took a wide loop around, bringing herself out near the riverbank, a kilometre upstream of where she'd left the Doctor and Ty. Poking her head out of the bushes, she pulled out her monocular and used it to scan downriver: she could see the buildings clearly, but there was no sign of the otters, the brainwashed settlers or the Doctor and Ty. She hoped that meant they'd got away.

So... where were the rest of the settlers? She'd had plenty of time to think as she'd made her way back, and it seemed only common sense that if they weren't at the settlement then they'd be somewhere else doing the creature's dirty work. And that surely had to mean the ship, the *One Small Step*...

Candy shuddered inwardly at the memory of finding Col and what he'd done to himself – all to stop the creature from finding out any more. But she – and, Candy suspected, Col too – reckoned it was probably too late.

After she'd realised that it was pointless trying to drag Col's body from the ship, she'd noticed the shipbrain's illuminated control panel; and, curious, she'd checked it out to see what could have brought Col all the way out here in secrecy.

What she saw puzzled – then angered – her: Col had been deleting records from the ship's memory. Pallister's records. It took her a few minutes to work out why. And when she did, the anger kicked in.

'Why, Col?' she'd whispered, scrolling through Pallister's records. 'Why d'you do it?'

Col had been deleting Pallister's history file – the record that had come with him aboard the ship. Normally only for the eyes of the ship's Captain and the previous Chief Councillor, both of whom had died in the flood, Pallister's history file seemed somewhat at odds with the picture of himself that he'd presented at the elections. Elections that

Col himself had been in charge of organising.

A few moments of thought and it was clear to Candy what Col had done: Pallister's history contained numerous convictions for petty crime, fraud and embezzlement. And yet none of that had been mentioned during the elections. Quite the reverse, in fact. The history file placed on *public* record, in the run-up to the election, had shown Pallister to be a model citizen, beyond reproach. A selfless, hardworking, dedicated man.

Col had helped to fix the election so that Pallister would win.

And then when news of the *One Small Step*'s return had reached Sunday City, Col must have panicked, thinking that someone might check the ship's records and discover that someone had fiddled with them. So he'd rushed out here to delete them, covering his – and Pallister's – tracks. Maybe Pallister himself had suggested it.

Was *that* what he'd been apologising about?

Col's words came back to her, sharply, as though he were speaking them now: 'Tell them I'm sorry,' he'd said. 'For letting it find out about Pallister.'

But *why*? It made no sense. Why would it matter whether the creature discovered that Pallister was a petty criminal and that his election had been fixed?

She was still puzzling over that as she hid in the bushes. Still puzzling over it, as the sound of her own breathing began to subside, and she heard a faint and distant noise. A low, mechanical droning, it drifted across the treetops from well beyond the far bank. And for a few moments she sat there wondering where she'd heard the noise before. Only when it finally came to her did she heave herself to her feet. She looked back towards Sunday City, wondering if the Doctor and Ty had heard the sound. But it was so faint that she wasn't even sure she was hearing it herself.

Quietly, she stepped into the open and began to make her way upstream, looking for a shallow crossing point, pausing every few metres to listen. And the more she listened, the more certain she became – and the more puzzled.

Why had someone decided to start up the drill?

On the other side of the forest, nearly two kilometres away from the original settlement, stood the spindly tower of the deep drill – a skeletal column of metal scaffolding over a hundred metres tall. Thirty metres away stood the drill's squat control room. And wandering between the two, silently, were the remaining kidnapped settlers.

And watching over them all in the darkness was the man that had once been Pallister. Suspended a metre above the ground, he hung like a broken doll above the water's edge, slick pipes of flesh still pumping chemicals in and out of his brain, feeding back to the thing that waited beneath the waters. There was no longer any real Pallister there. There hadn't been for a while – not since the Doctor had attacked it. Now he was just an encyclopaedia for the swamp creature to flick through at will, a database, a source of knowledge and information. Raw brainpower, tied directly in to the creature. Brainpower that the alien was putting to good use.

The thing controlling him held no bitterness, no anger. The Doctor's action had been understandable – he had sought to survive. The body that housed Pallister's brain had been damaged by what the Doctor had done, but the brain still functioned. After a fashion.

Even filtered through Pallister's senses and memories, the creature could make little sense of the Doctor's earlier questions. It simply could not comprehend how any creature could not understand life's prime directive: to reproduce, to make more, to colonise and spread.

There was nothing else.

'You know,' said the Doctor, his eyes sweeping grimly around the room, 'I'm half afraid that if I tell you that the worst thing, just at the moment, would be an army of killer robots with flashing red laser-beam eyes, someone would open a cupboard door and point out that you've already got one...'

He was seething, Martha could tell.

'Anyway...' He seemed to calm down a little. 'This drill: tell me more about it.'

A youngish man – early twenties, Martha guessed – with long, straggly blond hair raised a hand at the back of the crowd. 'It's for extracting low-grade uranium ore,' he said. 'The drill tower's a hundred metres tall, but the extensible bit can go as deep as five hundred. There's a reasonable seam of ore down there. The drill makes a hole and then we drop low-grade explosives down to fracture it.'

'And then leach it out with a chemical solution?' asked

the Doctor. 'And pump it back up to the surface for processing?'

The man nodded, his mouth tight, worried.

'So much for your intentions to switch to fusion power,' he said darkly, glancing at Ty. 'Looks like you've already got yourself a long-term energy policy.'

'But what's this got to do with that creature wanting to set off a nuclear bomb under our backsides?' Henig put in.

'Never heard of the Orion Project?' asked the Doctor. His eye caught Martha's. She gave a shrug.

'Today's been a real history lesson for you lot, hasn't it,' said the Doctor wearily. 'It was an idea,' he said eventually, 'back on Earth in the 1940s, for a nuclear pulse rocket. The idea was to build a big spaceship – a *really* big spaceship. Whopping, in fact. The size of a city. And to power it by setting off nuclear bombs under its bum.'

'And it worked?' This was Ty, eyes wide with disbelief.

'Oh, they never actually built it – too many practical problems. But in theory it could have done. The back end of the ship was nothing more than a huge steel plate, designed to absorb the radiation and act as a cushion, letting the energy of the bombs push the rocket forwards. A bit brutal for my tastes, but where would we be if everyone thought the same, eh?'

Henig shook his head. 'You're mad!' he said, looking around the crowd for agreement. 'You expect us to believe that this thing's going to take the power core from the ship, turn it into a bomb, drop it down the bore hole and then sit back and go surfboarding into space on a chunk of rock?'

'Oh, I've known people try to surfboard into space on far more unbelievable things,' the Doctor said. 'But yes – you've summed it up nicely, Henig.'

The Doctor pulled the sonic screwdriver from his pocket for the umpteenth time and waved it around. A faint blue light came from the tip and it emitted a feeble buzzing, like the sound of a dying fly. Henig and the other Sundayans were arguing about what the Doctor had told them. Martha couldn't quite tell which way it was going. Some of them had started crying. Others just shouted and banged their fists on tables, as if that would help.

The Doctor pulled a grumpy face and smacked the sonic screwdriver against the palm of his hand, examining the flecks of mud that came out.

'Listen,' Martha said, trying to change the subject. 'I've been thinking. Why don't we take a few people out into the swamp, find the TARDIS, and just give them all a lift back home? Problem solved! Then that thing can set off its bomb, and it won't matter. It can blow itself to kingdom come for all we'll care.' She gave him a bright, optimistic smile.

'And what if they don't want to go, eh? Have you asked them?'

'You think they're going to want to stay with slimey out there about to blow up half the planet? And even if it doesn't, they'd have to be mad to carry on living here, especially if we *can't* get rid of it.'

'These people have invested their whole lives in this place, Martha – the dead ones literally. They're not going to give up without a fight. And besides, if we let slimey blow its seeds into space, who knows what the next planet it infects is going to be.' He paused, pointedly. 'It could even be Earth. No, the fat lady's not even out of her dressing room yet, never mind started singing. And *we*,' he tapped her on the chin, 'are going to make sure that she can't find her costume.'

With perfect dramatic timing, Orlo came rushing into the room.

'They've started up the drill!' he gasped, steadying himself on the back of a chair as the settlers crowded round. 'I've just heard it! I wasn't sure at first, but...'

'Oh whoopty-doo,' said the Doctor tiredly. 'You know, I think the fat lady's just had her five-minute call.' He looked around the room, eyes suddenly narrow and thoughtful.

That's his 'Right! Time for a plan' face! thought Martha.

'Is there a geologist in the house?' asked the Doctor. 'Or a Sundayologist, I suppose. And not someone who studies ice creams, thank you Martha.'

Ha ha.

A stocky black guy with a weird, asymmetric beard stood up.

'Excellent!' said the Doctor. 'What's the ground like out there? Will the shaft need some clearing out?'

The man nodded. 'It's been untouched since before the flood,' he said. 'I reckon that it'll take 'em two or three hours to establish a proper shaft.'

'Buys us a bit of time,' the Doctor said thoughtfully, chewing on his lip.

The room fell quiet again, and it was Ty who broke the

silence. 'So you really think that dropping a bomb down the hole will protect the creature from the radiation and the blast?'

The Doctor shrugged, wide-eyed. 'Depends on the size of the bomb. Depends on the density of the ground. Depends on how strong that thing is. But it'll certainly give it more protection from the blast and the radiation than detonating it above ground.' He paused for a moment. 'But yes, I think it will. When that thing blows, there'll be a lot of damage. An *awful* lot of damage. But judging by the junior slimey that Martha brought back, there'll be more than enough bits of it left to colonise a thousand planets.'

'How easy is it, anyway, to build an atomic bomb?' asked Martha. 'Aren't they, like, quite technical?'

'Oh in principle they're very simple,' the Doctor replied, making two fists and holding them out at arm's length. 'You get a metal casing and two small lumps of uranium-235 along with a couple of explosive charges to slam them into each other.' He brought his fists together. 'When combined they create a critical mass. All you need is a bit of gubbins to hold it all in place, a bit more gubbins to act as a detonator – and *voilà*! Instant Armageddon!'

'*That* easy?' Martha was aghast.

'Well, OK, maybe not quite *that* easy – but well within the capabilities of people who are running their own nuclear reactor. Well within the capabilities of Pallister, I should imagine, and that's where slimey's getting his information from. It fits perfectly with the parts the settlers remembered fetching for it. And it's not like it's got to worry about protecting you lot from radiation.'

The Doctor turned to Orlo. 'I hate to ask,' he said, 'but we need someone out there to keep an eye on the otters even more than ever. If that creature *is* planning to drop an atomic bomb down the bore hole, we need as much warning as we can get.' He gripped Orlo by the shoulder. 'You up for it?'

Orlo grinned. 'Try and stop me!' he said.

'He's a good lad, that one,' the Doctor said as Orlo vanished. 'Common sense and enthusiasm – the best qualifications I can think of. Maybe you should make *him* the head of the Council when this is all over.'

'*If*,' said Ty.

'Oh, Professor Benson!' exclaimed the Doctor. 'Look on the bright side!'

'Anyway – how's that sonic doo-dah of yours? Cleaned it out yet? It's the only thing we've got that'll work against all those otters, remember.'

He fished the sonic screwdriver out of his pocket and gave it another go. The light was brighter this time, but it began to fade after a few moments. Desolately, he tossed it into the air and Martha caught it.

'Technology!' he snorted. 'It's all rubbish in the end, isn't it! Still, Professor Benson, we have something even better at our disposal, haven't we?'

'You're talking about your brain again, aren't you?' said Ty wryly.

His face fell. 'Am I that transparent?'

'As glass,' Ty grinned.

* * *

'What's the point of this?' asked Ty as she watched the Doctor power up the centrifuge. With a whine, it rattled up to speed whilst the Doctor rolled his sleeve back down and set the hypodermic back on the table.

'Plan B,' the Doctor said. 'Or Plan A, I suppose. Depending on whether I can come up with a Plan C.'

'What?' Ty was now totally confused.

The Doctor had dragged her over to the bio lab and, in a frenetic whirl of activity, had activated the tabletop display. He punched up dozens of different images of the proteins that he'd extracted from himself, Martha and the otters. She'd followed him around the room as he'd started up all sorts of pieces of equipment, transferring vials of fluids from one to another, running the results through the chromatograph and the sequencer, testing them again and then going through the whole process all over again. Martha had been sent off to see if she could find any plans or schematics of the drill site and information about the ship's power cores.

The Doctor's final step had been the most frightening: with a cry of 'Yes!' he'd taken the last test tube of straw-coloured fluid, filled a hypodermic with it – and jabbed it into his own arm.

'What the *future* are you doing?' she cried, reaching out to snatch the syringe from him. But she was too late. He closed his eyes, leaned back against the table and gave a deep sigh.

'Shush,' he said softly, raising a finger. 'The Doctor-o-tronic needs shush. *Biiiig* shush.'

Ty glared at him. How could he be so *stupid*? Hadn't he

learned anything from what had happened last night? From what he'd said back in the Council chamber, they were only a couple of hours away from a nuclear holocaust, and here he was injecting alien proteins into himself. Again.

'Doctor?' she ventured after a few minutes. It seemed that he'd stopped breathing altogether. His body was motionless, still seated on the video table, leaning back at an angle. 'Doctor?'

His eyes flicked open and Ty flinched. He was staring straight ahead, and although the whites of his eyes were still visible, his irises were completely black. Flecks of dark green and brown swirled in them like grains of dust in a sunbeam. A chill crept down Ty's spine.

Not again, she thought. *Please… not again…*

Orlo raised the monocular to his eye and scanned the drill site.

Its location had meant that it had avoided the flooding that wiped out the first Sunday City. And it hadn't been used since then: there was enough power left in the ship's spare core to keep the new settlement going for another year. The settlers had enough on their plates without worrying about mining more uranium just yet. And they'd built a smaller, wood-fired station to cope with the nuclear plant's occasional downtimes.

But there was no doubt – the kidnapped settlers were operating the deep drill. And, all around them, the creepy figures of the otters stood guard.

Orlo wished he'd thought to ask the Doctor what a bomb

might look like. But he didn't imagine it would be so small that he might miss it.

Suddenly, out of the corner of his eye, Orlo caught a flash of movement. Bringing the monocular back up to his eye, he searched for it again. There – in the shadow behind the drill control room. It couldn't be… He twisted the zoom ring on the monocular and the image jumped about before steadying.

Kneeling at the base of the building was an unmistakeable figure. Candy.

Candy's heart was pounding as she pressed herself into the corner behind the control room. All the otters and the settlers, as far as she could tell, were busy around the front – on the drill tower itself and in and out of the squat grey building behind her.

She'd shuffled her way closer and closer to the drill site, convinced that this was something the settlers and the Doctor needed to know about. Why would they want to be drilling? What use could they have for uranium? The *One Small Step* was surely beyond repair, so they couldn't be trying to get fuel for it.

From where she was hiding, all she could see was the top of the tower, a skinny metal finger pointing at the orange sky. And then suddenly something glinted: a brief flash of light from the undergrowth at the edge of the clearing. Fishing in her backpack, she pulled out her monocular and raised it to her eye.

Grinning at her and waving, buried in the shadows of the

bushes, was Orlo – watching her watching him.

'What's going on?' asked Martha suspiciously as she burst into the main bio lab. It was the only place she could think of that the Doctor might have gone – and she was right. He was fiddling around with tubes of liquids and pipettes in his shirt sleeves whilst Ty watched him, her arms folded sullenly. There was definitely an atmosphere in the room.

'What?' said the Doctor with a forced brightness as he took a test tube out of a clunky-looking old centrifuge and held it up to the light. He was wearing his glasses again, and the harsh fluorescent light glanced off them, making his eyes unreadable.

'You rushed off,' Martha said. 'I didn't know where you'd gone. We found some plans and what-not. They're looking them over back in the Council chamber. For all the good it'll do. What's all this then?' Martha indicated the video table, lit up like a Christmas tree, images of molecules and proteins all over its glossy surface. One or two of them were coloured in shades of red – a warning if ever there was one.

'Belt and braces,' the Doctor said with another false smile.

'You're up to something, aren't you?'

'Me?'

'What's that?' Martha indicated the yellowish liquid that the Doctor was now pouring into a little glass and metal cartridge.

He frowned and looked up at the ceiling, as if the answer to her question was written there.

'Plan D, I think.' He flashed a grin at Ty. 'Or was it E?'

Ty glared at him and now Martha was certain something was up. There was an atmosphere in the room – half conspiracy, half just-had-a-blazing-row. Martha used to think that she didn't do jealousy, but there was something about the way he seemed to be confiding in Ty that got her hackles up. Again.

The Doctor was filling another of the little cartridges. 'Right,' he said, tossing the capsules into the air with one hand and catching them neatly in the other. He took off his glasses, swiped up his jacket from the back of a chair and slipped it on. 'No time like the present. And if we don't hurry, there really won't be.'

And, with that, he slipped past the two of them and through the doors.

SIXTEEN

- .... . -.-- | .- .-. . | ... . -. -. | - ..... . | -... .-. .. .-.. .-.. | ..--.. | | -.. --- -.
- | -.-.-. --- .-- | .-- .... .-.. | ..--.. | | .. -- | --. .-- .. -. -. | - --- | .... .- -...
--- - .-. .-. .--. . | .. -

'You're mad,' Orlo whispered to himself. 'You're completely raving mad.'

The flashes from Candy's torch ceased, and he saw her wave at him and slip it into her backpack. He hoped he'd understood her Morse code message. If he'd remembered to bring his own torch with him, he'd have told her what he thought of her plan – and what the Doctor had said about the creature's plan. As he watched her through the monocular, she crouched down in the shadow of the building and began to inch her way around to the window.

If someone had told Martha Jones, just a few weeks ago, that she'd find herself heading deliberately towards a nuclear bomb, she'd have laughed them out of the room. And yet here she was, on a swampy alien planet, light years from

Earth, doing just that.

It put the rest of her life in perspective.

And it might just end it.

'What if we can't stop it?' she whispered to the Doctor, hoping that Ty couldn't hear her.

'Oh, we'll stop it.' He sounded quietly confident. He *always* sounded quietly confident. Well, sometimes noisily confident. But always confident.

'Why are you doing this?' It was Ty.

'Because if we don't,' answered the Doctor breezily, 'then slimey-boy wins, and we lose. And if I have one fault, it's that I'm not a good loser.'

'You sound like you do this kind of thing often.'

'More often than is healthy, believe me,' said Martha, pushing a branch aside as they started up the slope that would bring them out above the drill site. A rustle of bushes further along the slope caught their eyes.

'It's Orlo!' whispered Ty.

Martha looked where she was pointing, and could just make out his stocky frame, his back to them, squatting in the undergrowth.

'Go and get him,' urged the Doctor gently. 'If this *doesn't* work out, I want him as far away from here as possible.'

Ty squeezed the Doctor's hand and went to get Orlo.

Look before you leap.

That's what people had always told Candy. They'd never given her the *He who hesitates is lost* one. Candy had *never* been given warnings about hesitating.

She wished, just now, that someone had.

The idea that had suddenly struck her as she'd waved goodbye to Orlo was just *so* obvious.

So obvious, in fact, that she kept thinking that there must be an equally obvious reason why it wouldn't work. A really obvious reason that would jump up and bite her, like a 'gator out of the swamp, when it was too late. Making sure that no one could see her, hiding in the shadow at the corner of the building, she slowly stood upright – and stepped out into the light.

And then, keeping her face fixed and flabby like the other settlers, she began to walk.

In Candy's panicky head, it was perfect. The other Sundayans were acting on instructions that the slime-thing had given them earlier. So were the otters. The slime-thing wasn't actually remote-controlling them, not in real-time. So there was no reason why, if she didn't act threatening, any of them should react to her. They'd see her – if they saw her at all – as just another zombie. Her legs were shaking like jelly as she slowly threaded her way through the others and around the building to the doorway. Not even risking a *tiny* look back, she walked inside.

The room was cool and dim – no one had bothered to turn on the lights. But there was enough illumination from the windows to see what was happening. Dory Chan was motionless by a big desk on which, unrolled, was a schematic of the drill mechanism and shaft. Dory was staring into space as if she'd done what she was programmed for and was waiting for further instructions. That didn't make sense, surely, thought Candy as she moved alongside her. Hadn't the Doctor said that when the slime creature's instructions had been completed the settlers and the otters had to go back to it for more? That could only mean one thing: that the slime creature had no more instructions for Dory. And if it had no more instructions, then it had no more use for her.

Candy snuck a glance out of the window. All around, the settlers were coming to a halt. She saw Eton, Pallister's aide, walking in stuttery circles. The otters were all stationary.

And then she saw movement.

One of the quad bikes was being pushed along by three of the settlers. The engine wasn't running and on the cart at the back was big, grey cylinder almost as big as the engine of the quad bike itself. The cylinder was strapped up with metaltape and looked, thought Candy, a right dog's dinner. Following on behind were two more settlers, pushing a huge reel of grey electrical cable, unrolling it along the ground as they went. What were they doing? She followed the line of the cable – and realised that it snaked in through the window of the control centre in which she stood. *Just like that tentacle had snaked in through the window of the ship. The tentacle that had attached itself to Col. The tentacle that had killed him.*

Candy ran to the cable and followed its route. It ended in a large, locking plug on a control panel. Quickly, she grabbed it and tried to turn it. But it was fixed tight. A keyed collar held it in place. Frantically, she wrenched at it with her bare hands, but it was no use. It wasn't budging.

Think! She told herself, trying to make sense of it all. She remembered what the Doctor had told her: common sense. Think things through a step at a time… The slime-thing had control of the settlers, and the settlers were about to drop something down the drill shaft. Therefore, whatever it was had to be bad. She had to find a way to—

Her train of thought was derailed as something moved in the shadows of the control room. *Several* somethings. Her mouth went dry and she froze as, out of the darkness, an otter appeared, its beady eyes fixed on her. Silently, another one appeared, and then another.

Within seconds, she was surrounded.

The Doctor clenched his fists and stared out over the drill site. So close…

Down on the mud around the old settlement stood the kidnapped settlers. One or two of them had fallen over and were lying motionless on the ground. Scattered between them were the otters – and some of them looked like they were sleeping too.

The only movement was at the base of the drill tower.

He squinted. He could hardly make out what was going on. Three of the settlers had pushed one of the quad bikes up to the base of the drill. On the back was something fat and cylindrical – it could only be the bomb. Behind it, two more had unrolled a huge drum of cabling, letting it spool out loosely on the mud – yards and yards and yards of it, back to the Nerve Centre. Even if he ran down there at full tilt, it'd be too late now.

As he watched, the settlers heaved at the bomb and it

tumbled from the back of the bike – and vanished out of sight into the drill shaft.

Like battery-operated toys whose power had just run out, the settlers fell over and lay still. The cable, looped on the ground in great scribbly swirls, began to unravel, following it down the hole.

'We're too late,' said the Doctor softly, a bleakness in his voice that Martha had never heard before. 'They've done it. They've dropped the bomb.'

Without looking round, he reached out to his side and found Martha's hand. If this was how it ended, then it would be like this. The two of them. Together.

'It's been fun,' he whispered, looking down at her.

He felt her fingers tighten in his.

'The best,' Martha said without a trace of sadness. 'Smith and Jones.'

'Smith and Jones.'

There wasn't anything else to say.

In silence, they waited.

And waited.

And, just for good measure, they waited a bit more.

'Maybe it's still falling,' Martha ventured.

'Maybe it is.'

So they waited *just* a bit more. Until the end of the cable – the end that, really, should have been plugged into a little box with a great big handle on the top – flicked into sight like a snake's tongue – and vanished down the hole after the bomb.

'You know,' said the Doctor slowly, as if trying not to

be *too* presumptuous, 'I always said the Chinese did the best fireworks displays.' He glanced at Martha. 'This one's *rubbish*, isn't it?'

And before she could say anything, he grabbed her in a whopping great hug and lifted her off her feet, swinging her round in the air a full three turns, before plonking her back on the ground, still laughing.

'Like I always say,' he grinned like a loon. 'Technology – it's all rubbish in the end!'

'What happened?' Martha said eventually, as dizzy from the hug as she was from the realisation that the bomb hadn't gone off – and wasn't going to.

'At a guess, I'd say our moist little friend forgot to plug something in. Either that, or—'

He stopped as the sound of an elephant crashing through the forest broke the silence. Both of them jumped as Ty and Orlo stumbled out of the bushes. With a huge grin, he gave them both a hug – but not, thought Martha, as big as the hug he'd given her. Instantly, she felt cheap for even noticing.

'Candy,' Orlo panted.

'It's just food, food, food with you, isn't it?' said the Doctor, rolling his eyes. 'Hang on – I might have a biscuit here somewh—'

Orlo shook his head, catching his breath. 'No,' he said. 'Candy. *Candy*.'

'Candice? What about her?'

'She… she did it.' Orlo pointed a trembling hand towards the drill site.

'Candice did what…?' Realisation suddenly dawned on

him. 'Candice did *that*? She sabotaged the bomb?'

And as if Candy had heard him, a little face appeared around the side of the building, peering cautiously up at them.

'Candice Kane!' bellowed the Doctor. 'Get yourself up here! Now! There's a serious hugging waiting for you!'

Ty couldn't believe it – somehow Candy had stopped the bomb. And with just seconds to spare. She watched as the girl raced up the slope towards them.

But she wasn't alone: seconds later, she was followed by a tiny, scampering procession of otters. For a moment, Ty froze, wondering whether the Doctor's sonic doohickey had recharged. But then she noticed something about one of the otters: the grey, smudgy patch on one ear. These were *her* otters.

Candy skidded and slipped a few times in her haste, but soon she was with them and they threw their arms around her, squeezing her until she squealed. The otters lined up a few yards away, holding each other's paws like well-behaved junior school kids.

Orlo gave her an embarrassed hug too. 'Your spelling's terrible,' he said with a grin.

Candy pulled a *uh?* face.

'Your Morse code,' Orlo explained. 'How d'you spell "sabotage" again?'

She punched him playfully on the arm.

'What did you do, though?' asked the Doctor, clearly still puzzled, his eyes flicking to the silent line of otters, all looking up at them expectantly.

'Common sense,' grinned Candy. 'Like you said. I thought it through. Whatever that thing was dropping down the drill shaft had to be bad, didn't it? And when I saw the cable it was trailing, I tried to unplug it. Only it was locked in – and then these guys turned up.' She turned and smiled at the otters, which made appreciative squeeing noises, dancing from one foot to the other at the attention they were getting. 'I thought I'd had it – that they were going to attack me or something. And then…' She smiled and shook her head. 'They started talking. Can you believe it? *Talking!* "We help," they said. "We help!" Thought I was going mad but then I thought, "What the heck." What did I have to lose? So I pointed to the cable. It was unravelling but there was still a lot of slack in it. And I told them to cut it.

'And before I knew it, they'd jumped on it and were chewing at it like mad.' A shadow of guilt passed across her face. 'I didn't think, 'til afterwards, that it might be electrified.'

'Nah,' said the Doctor. 'Only needed a tiny trigger signal.'

'Lucky for them,' Ty said.

'Lucky for *us*,' Martha added.

'Trigger signal?' Candy looked puzzled. 'Trigger for what? What was that thing – a nuclear bomb or something?' She laughed.

The Doctor gave a shrug. And a wink. 'Something like that,' he said.

* * *

But the feelgood factor didn't last. Once she thought about it, Martha realised it wouldn't.

'We've got to get down there, and quick,' the Doctor said, suddenly fired up. 'We need to take that drill apart – with our bare hands if necessary – before slimey realises that his little firecracker's turned into a damp squib. And we need to get the settlers out of there. They'll be waking up soon and I don't want slimey to get another shot at them.'

'It'll try again?' Ty was aghast.

'Wouldn't you? It nearly worked the first time, and once it works out what went wrong, it's bound to think about giving it another go. When the taxi for Mr Slime doesn't arrive, it'll poke its nose out, interface with an otter or two and work out what went wrong. And then it'll have another go. There's still the power core back in Sunday City's generator station, remember? Come on!'

And before anyone could say anything, the Doctor was scrambling down the bank towards the drill.

'How long will it take before they start moving?' Ty whispered, as they threaded their way between the motionless otters.

'Minutes,' the Doctor said. 'Hours, maybe. Depends when they were last in contact with slimey. As the proteins in their brains break down, they'll go back to being just otters.'

One or two of them twitched slightly as the five of them made their way across the open ground. Little limbs paddled the air, like dreaming cats. Martha jumped as one close to her gave a tiny, plaintive *squee*. The others, the friendly ones, had stayed well clear at the Doctor's instruction: if slimey decided to make a reappearance (and they were all still worryingly close to the water), he didn't want them getting caught by it.

'This is creepy,' Martha muttered, and Orlo grabbed her hand. 'If you're wrong and they suddenly wake up, Doctor, we're in big trouble.'

'Nah,' he said casually. 'When they wake up they're going to be just like they were before slimey arrived. They'll be smart and friendly, just like your little pals back there. And this time, hopefully, they'll have the common sense to stay away from the water.'

'You better be right,' she said as they reached the control room. 'Where do we start?' She stopped suddenly, aware of a sound she hadn't heard before: a soft scraping sound, like a heavy body being dragged across dry soil.

Orlo clearly heard it too. 'What's that?' he whispered as the five of them froze. Martha saw that the Doctor was looking up towards the roof of the control room.

'It's the man with the matches,' he said softly. 'Come to see why his firework display didn't go off.'

Moving over the roof and descending rapidly towards them was the puppet-like form of Pallister, still suspended from the throbbing green tendrils buried in his skull. His flesh was even more disgusting, more decayed than before. And as the swamp creature lowered him, Martha could see the bones of his right hand and arm showing through the rotted flesh. The right leg was missing at the hip.

'Back away,' muttered the Doctor fiercely, pushing Martha

behind him. 'Move. *Now!*'

Martha turned instinctively – only to see a shimmering tide of green-black flesh oozing around the sides of the control centre like a huge hand reaching out for them.

'You have interfered,' came the creature's voice from Pallister's mouth. It was hardly recognisable as a voice at all, so damaged was the man's body. Martha could see the bloated, black tongue lolling out over his lips, the jet-black eyes transfixing her with their dead stare. 'The spawning time is here and you have interfered. You will interfere no more.'

And with that, two huge tongues of oily flesh licked out from around the building and lunged for them.

SEVENTEEN

'**W**ait!' shouted the Doctor, raising his hands. 'Wait! Listen to me!'

'Oh yeah,' said Martha scathingly. 'That's going to w—'

She stopped, mid-sentence, as she saw, miraculously, the tendril pause in mid-air, hovering like it had done in front of her back in the otters' nest. Orlo, Ty and Candy were staring at it in silent horror.

'Why?' said Pallister slowly.

'Because I can help you,' the Doctor said.

'You what?' Martha found herself saying.

'Shush!' the Doctor snapped without turning round. 'I can help you find other planets to colonise,' the Doctor said loudly, addressing Pallister. 'That's what you want, isn't it? To blow yourself into pieces, to give your children a lovely little start in life, eh? Well let me help.'

There was a moment's silence.

'How?'

Martha saw the tentacles flick lazily in the air, like lizard's tongues, as if they were tasting the Doctor's statements for truth.

'My spaceship – the TARDIS.'

'What is that?' asked Pallister, his voice flat and dead.

'It's how I got here – how I came to this planet. A blue box. You've seen it: you pulled Martha out of it, remember, under the water? The otters picked up the image of it from you.'

'This…?' said Pallister. And, before their eyes, the tip of the tendril reshaped itself into a rough, featureless approximation of the TARDIS.

'That's it!' cried the Doctor eagerly. 'You know where it is – if you get it out of the swamp, I can use it to take your little slimey babies to a dozen planets.' He shrugged. 'Why just a dozen? Make it a hundred – no, a thousand! I can spread your children across the galaxy better than you could ever do yourself. None of that wasting ninety-nine per cent of them just for the sake of the one per cent that land near a good school.'

It's a trick, thought Martha instantly. There was no way the Doctor would offer to help the creature infect other planets, other worlds. Not even to save *her*. He'd trap it in the TARDIS or eject it into the sun. Something like that. She'd seen what he'd done with the Family, back in 1913.

'Why?' came the rasping gurgle from Pallister's mouth.

'Why? Because I'm like that – always stopping for hitch-hikers, aren't I, Martha? And because it's the only way to make you leave this planet – and leave these people.'

Pallister just stared at them – or the creature behind it did.

Martha had no idea whether it understood the concept of a double-cross. If it was filtering everything through what was left of Pallister's brain, it must have known the Doctor might be trying to trick it.

But maybe it was like the Doctor had said earlier: instinct versus intelligence. Perhaps the creature's instinct to reproduce was just so strong, its own intelligence so pitiful, that it wouldn't be able to see beyond its own blind drive to make more swamp creatures, to fill the universe with copies of itself. Was this some bizarre, twisted version of motherhood (or fatherhood, she supposed)? Is this how any parent would be when faced with the survival of its kids? People went to such lengths to have babies back on Earth, didn't they? Not that most people would condemn a whole world for one. But still… It was a powerful drive.

'Yes,' said Pallister suddenly.

Without warning, the green tendril that still held the shape of the TARDIS flowed out into a grasping funnel and clamped itself around the Doctor's head. Ty screamed and staggered back.

'Yes,' repeated Pallister soullessly as the rope of alien flesh spread out and began to engulf him. 'You will help me. You will be me. I will take the TARDIS. I will be everywhere. Now… *show me how!*'

'No!' yelled Martha, racing after the Doctor as the creature began to pull him back across the mud, his dragging heels carving soft gouges into it. She pounded her fists against the creature's hide, but it was as hard and unyielding as it had been in the otters' nest. Through the translucent flesh, threaded with dark veins, she could see the Doctor's features – his mouth open in horror, his eyes wide. It was spreading slowly down over his shoulders, like gelatinous oil, smothering him. His legs were kicking frantically, mud spattering everywhere, and she knew it was only seconds before he passed out through lack of oxygen. Even now the thing would be trying to insinuate itself into his mouth, his nose, his ears. She caught sight of his eyes for just a moment.

'Stand back!' someone ordered.

Martha turned. It was Ty, and she was holding a tiny gun. 'What–'

The words stuck in Martha's throat as she watched Ty expertly snap two glass and metal cartridges into the top of it – the same cartridges she'd seen the Doctor filling with liquid back in the bio lab. Why had Ty got it?

'I said stand back!' Ty shouted again, raising the gun and gripping it with both hands.

'What are you doing?' Martha yelled, refusing to move.

'Plan A,' Ty said grimly – and fired.

There was a soft *pht* of compressed air, and Martha spun to see a feathered dart bounce harmlessly off the creature's flesh and fall to the ground. She glanced up to see Ty looking straight at her.

'Just checking,' she said, and lowered the aim of the gun a little. For some reason, her brown eyes were filling with tears. 'I'm sorry, Martha. I'm so sorry.'

For a second, Martha heard an echo of the Doctor's own voice in Ty's – the times he'd apologised to others, for things done to them that he had no control over; things that he felt, maybe, he could have stopped.

In that second, Martha realised what Ty was doing – if the poisoned dart couldn't penetrate the creature's flesh, there was only one way to get it into its system.

Through the Doctor.

Martha leaped forwards. 'No way! You can't!' she cried.

But it was too late. She could almost see the dart leave the tranquilliser gun. Almost see it as it trailed through the air.

In silence, it buried itself in the Doctor's leg.

Martha sank to her knees as the creature continued to envelop the Doctor. The tide of alien flesh rolled lower, down over his thighs and over the dart. His body twitched as if he were still fighting against the creature's grip.

If the poison were strong enough to kill the creature, Martha knew, then the Doctor was as good as dead. She'd seen what had happened to Pallister when the Doctor had shot him before. And for this one to have any real effect on the creature it had to be ten – no, a hundred! – times as strong.

Martha watched as the swamp creature cocooned the Doctor, like a fly caught in green amber. His struggles suddenly ceased, his body flopping limply in the creature's grasp. Silently, the alien monstrosity continued to drag him across the mud to the corner of the building, towards the water.

And then, suddenly, it stopped, and a weird change came over it. Like condensation on a cold glass of beer, the surface of the creature's skin began to frost over.

Martha stared, puzzled, unable to understand what she was looking at. The cloudiness began to spread from the area of the Doctor's head, like a wave, radiating outwards. It spread down as far as the Doctor's feet, still protruding, almost comically, from the alien flesh. And then, with a horrid ripping sound, the creature's tendril *burst*, showering her with warm, slimy goo, and the Doctor fell heavily to the ground, gasping and choking.

Ty was at his side instantly, Orlo and Candy just a second behind, pulling the stuff from his face and out of his mouth. Martha just knelt there, stunned, as he coughed the alien muck up.

Behind him, the massive bulk of the swamp creature's tendril had flopped to the ground, thrashing and writhing. It smacked against the side of the building, spattering it with dark slime. Martha watched as the wave of frostiness continuing to spread out over its surface, back towards the creature's body, hidden in the water; more and more of the alien's body fluids pumped out across the soil, like an out-of-control garden hose.

There was a dull thud beside her, and she turned to see Pallister's body sprawled out on the ground like a discarded toy: the tendrils that had supported it had burst, and greeny-black ichor was gushing everywhere.

Then Candy was beside her, helping her to her feet, and Orlo and Ty were dragging the Doctor away from the dying alien.

* * *

When they were clear of the spurting, bubbling fluid, Ty and Orlo lay the Doctor on the ground. Martha rushed to his side and cradled his slime-covered body in her arms. He coughed in her ear and tried to push her away. But Martha was having none of it. She held onto him until Ty gently prised her away.

'I'm not sure which was worse,' the Doctor choked, trying to sit up, wiping his face with his hands. 'Being smothered by slimey, or being smothered by you.' He looked up at her and grinned stupidly. 'Actually,' he said. 'It was no contest. Hello, Martha – you don't half look different through green glasses, you know.'

And then he fainted clean away.

EIGHTEEN

'But why didn't the poison kill him?' Martha said as she finished wiping the slime from his face.

'It wasn't a poison,' Ty said, tossing the tranquilliser gun to the ground and fixing it with a look of disgust.

'But it killed that thing – didn't it?'

'Actually,' said the Doctor muzzily, opening his eyes. 'I'm rather afraid you'll find that *I* killed it.'

'So what was in the dart?' Martha was confused.

'A rather clever little solution of RNA.' He sat up and rubbed the back of his head – before examining the goo on his hand and pulling a disgusted face. Before Martha could stop him, he sniffed his hand and gave it a lick. 'Ew!' he said. 'Needs more salt.'

'Stop it,' Martha chided, slapping his hand away from his face. 'What did you do?'

'Well it all seems a bit obvious now.'

'Not to me it doesn't. Stop being smug.'

He peered past her to where the remains of the creature

were nothing more than a huge, dark stain on the ground. Shreds of greeny-black flesh lay all around like the tattered pieces of a burst balloon.

'Slimey, there, controlled other organisms with proteins – injected them into them along with RNA to transfer memories and images. So it occurred to me that it might work the other way round: if I could get the right proteins and RNA *inside* it, I might be able to, well, mess about with its metabolism a bit.'

'I told him it was dangerous,' insisted Ty, as if trying to absolve herself of some guilt. 'I warned him.'

'She did,' the Doctor admitted. 'That's why I couldn't tell you, Martha – I knew you'd stop me.'

'So this RNA… I mean…' Martha was at a loss for words. This was all coming too thick and too fast. '*How?*'

'The marvellous Doctor-o-tronic!' he beamed up at her. 'I told you I was the best biological computer around. I had to make direct contact with the creature to be able to work on its metabolism – that's why I offered it the TARDIS.' His expression became suddenly more serious. 'I knew it wouldn't be able to resist, and that it would try to take control of me like it did poor old Pallister. But I had to give it the option. There always has to be a way out. Just a shame that people don't take it when it's offered.' He shrugged. 'Ah well. Anyway, it's had so much practice now that it knew exactly what to do with me. Well, it *thought* it did. It started to invade my body, and when it did, *I* invaded *its* body and reprogrammed the RNA string that Ty injected into me to destroy its outer membranes.' He grinned again, back to his jokey self. 'Didn't they teach you anything at medical school?'

'He couldn't have injected it into himself earlier,' Ty said. 'In case it broke down too quickly – or the creature detected it and neutralised it. It had to be at the very last minute.' Ty sighed and shook her head. 'I'm sorry I frightened you Martha, honey, really I am.'

Martha shook her head. If it hadn't worked… 'You *ever* do that again,' she said sternly to him, 'and you really *will* need a doctor. Believe me.'

'Your bedside manner leaves a lot to be desired, Miss Jones,' he smiled. 'But you're getting there. One day you'll make a great doctor.'

'With you about,' said Martha, shaking her head 'who needs another one?'

'Col rigged the election for Pallister?' Martha asked, as Candy explained what she'd found aboard the *One Small Step*. 'Why? It's not like there was anything in it for him, was there?'

They were making their way, wearily, back to the settlement. The sky had clouded over and the rain was beginning to fall. Again.

Ty shrugged. 'I think he just needed someone to believe in, someone to follow. And I guess we all need someone like that, don't we? Col's parents had guided him all his life, and out here I think he felt a bit at sea, so to speak. Pallister offered him some certainties, some structure. I think he was just doing the wrong thing for the right reasons. Or maybe that should be the other way around.'

'And once he'd fiddled the election,' Candy said, 'he couldn't go back. He wasn't a bad man,' she added after a pause. 'Just a misguided one.'

'That was how slimey got to find out about Pallister,' the Doctor said. 'Pallister must have been at the front of poor Col's mind when he got caught. So straight away slimey knew about the ship's power core and bombs and what-have-you.' He glanced at Ty. 'And I take it, Professor Benson, that there's going to be no more capturing and caging the jubjubs?'

'The *what?*' said Martha.

'The otters,' said Ty firmly.

The Doctor pulled an *I-give-up* face.

'No, there isn't,' Ty finished. 'If I'd known they were as smart as that, I'd never have done it in the first place. And *talking!* How come I never heard them talk before?'

The Doctor threw a glance at Martha.

'Blame us for that one,' he said. 'You might find that when we're gone, they're not quite so chatty. But there's nothing to stop you from trying. Come up with a completely new language, something you both can understand: imagine how that'd go down in the history books. You could call it Tyrellian. Or *ottyrellian.*' He paused and pulled a lemon-sucking face. 'Nah. Maybe not. Just show them a bit of respect – after all, they were here first – and who knows…? This could be the start of a beautiful friendship.'

'Something you know all about, eh, Doctor?'

Martha caught Ty's eye as she said it, and smiled.

'Oh yes,' said the Doctor breezily. 'Beautiful friendships.

You can never have enough of those, can you, Martha?'

'No, Doctor,' said Martha dutifully, returning Ty's smile, 'you can't.'

Martha and Ty fell back a little as Candy and the Doctor strode ahead.

'High maintenance,' Ty said, indicating the Doctor.

Martha laughed. 'You said it.'

'But worth it, honey.'

'You reckon?'

Ty pulled a face. 'You don't?'

Martha could only shrug, smiling.

'Trust your instincts,' Ty said. 'Isn't that what the Doctor told Candy? Just trust your instincts. That's all any of us can do.'

And striding into Sunday City, Martha felt Ty's arm across her shoulders.

At the edge of the forest, watching them go, stood a dozen otters, their paws interlinked.

'I like the tall one,' said one of them – the one with a soft, grey smudge on its ear.

'Oh, the one with the yellow fur's my favourite,' said another.

'They are kind of cute, aren't they?' said a third, a little wistfully.

'And easier to train than I'd thought, even if they are a bit dim!'

There was a chorus of nods and giggles.

'Still,' said the first one, 'intelligence isn't everything.

Come on – I want to see their spaceship!'

'Oooh yes! They've got a brain in a box. Let's go and play with it.'

And, still holding hands, the otters scampered back to the swamp.

These humans were going to be *fun!*

Acknowledgements

Thanks to Justin Richards, and to Gary Russell and everyone in Cardiff for having faith in me – hope I've done you proud.

And, as ever, big hugs to all my lovely proof-monkeys: Simon Forward, Mags Halliday, Mike Robinson, Paul Dale Smith and Nick Wallace; to Simon Bucher-Jones for sums and science; to Steve Tribe for finding last-minute problems – and solutions; and to Paul Magrs and Mark Morris for their help and support. New writers, new friends!

THE STONE ROSE
by Jacqueline Rayner

THE FEAST OF THE DROWNED
by Stephen Cole

THE RESURRECTION CASKET
by Justin Richards

THE NIGHTMARE OF BLACK ISLAND
by Mike Tucker

THE ART OF DESTRUCTION
by Stephen Cole

THE PRICE OF PARADISE
by Colin Brake

Also available from BBC Books
featuring the Doctor and Martha
as played by David Tennant and Freema Agyeman:

Sting of the Zygons

by Stephen Cole

ISBN 978 1 84607 225 3

UK £6.99 US $11.99/$14.99 CDN

The TARDIS lands the Doctor and Martha in the Lake District in 1909, where a small village has been terrorised by a giant, scaly monster. The search is on for the elusive 'Beast of Westmorland', and explorers, naturalists and hunters from across the country are descending on the fells. King Edward VII himself is on his way to join the search, with a knighthood for whoever finds the Beast.

But there is a more sinister presence at work in the Lakes than a mere monster on the rampage, and the Doctor is soon embroiled in the plans of an old and terrifying enemy. As the hunters become the hunted, a desperate battle of wits begins – with the future of the entire world at stake…

The Last Dodo

by Jacqueline Rayner

ISBN 978 1 84607 224 6

UK £6.99 US $11.99/$14.99 CDN

The Doctor and Martha go in search of a real live dodo, and are transported by the TARDIS to the mysterious Museum of the Last Ones. There, in the Earth section, they discover every extinct creature up to the present day, all still alive and in suspended animation.

Preservation is the museum's only job – collecting the last of every endangered species from all over the universe. But exhibits are going missing…

Can the Doctor solve the mystery before the museum's curator adds the last of the Time Lords to her collection?

DOCTOR·WHO
Wooden Heart
by Martin Day

ISBN 978 1 84607 226 0
UK £6.99 US $11.99/$14.99 CDN

A vast starship, seemingly deserted and spinning slowly in the void of deep space. Martha and the Doctor explore this drifting tomb, and discover that they may not be alone after all…

Who survived the disaster that overcame the rest of the crew? What continues to power the vessel? And why has a stretch of wooded countryside suddenly appeared in the middle of the craft?

As the Doctor and Martha journey through the forest, they find a mysterious, fogbound village – a village traumatised by missing children and prophecies of its own destruction.

Forever Autumn

by Mark Morris

ISBN 978 1 84607 270 3

UK £6.99 US $11.99/$14.99 CDN

It is almost Halloween in the sleepy New England town of Blackwood Falls. Autumn leaves litter lawns and sidewalks, paper skeletons hang in windows, and carved pumpkins leer from stoops and front porches.

The Doctor and Martha soon discover that something long dormant has awoken in the town, and this will be no ordinary Halloween. What is the secret of the ancient tree and the mysterious book discovered tangled in its roots? What rises from the local churchyard in the dead of night, sealing up the lips of the only witness? And why are the harmless trappings of Halloween suddenly taking on a creepy new life of their own?

As nightmarish creatures prowl the streets, the Doctor and Martha must battle to prevent both the townspeople and themselves from suffering a grisly fate…

Sick Building

by Paul Magrs

ISBN 978 1 84607 269 7

UK £6.99 US $11.99/$14.99 CDN

Tiermann's World: a planet covered in wintry woods and roamed by sabre-toothed tigers and other savage beasts. The Doctor is here to warn Professor Tiermann, his wife and their son that a terrible danger is on its way.

The Tiermanns live in luxury, in a fantastic, futuristic, fully-automated Dreamhome, under an impenetrable force shield. But that won't protect them from the Voracious Craw. A gigantic and extremely hungry alien creature is heading remorselessly towards their home. When it gets there everything will be devoured.

Can they get away in time? With the force shield cracking up, and the Dreamhome itself deciding who should or should not leave, things are looking desperate…

In March 2005, a 900-year-old alien in a police public call box made a triumphant return to our television screens. *The Inside Story* takes us behind the scenes to find out how the series was commissioned, made and brought into the twenty-first century. Gary Russell has talked extensively to everyone involved in the show, from the Tenth Doctor himself, David Tennant, and executive producer Russell T Davies, to the people normally hidden inside monster suits or behind cameras. Everyone has an interesting story to tell.

The result is the definitive account of how the new *Doctor Who* was created. With exclusive access to design drawings, backstage photographs, costume designs and other previously unpublished pictures, *The Inside Story* covers the making of all twenty-six episodes of Series One and Two, plus the Christmas specials, as well as an exclusive look ahead to the third series.

DOCTOR·WHO
Creatures and Demons

by Justin Richards

ISBN 978 1 84607 229 1

UK £7.99 US $12.99/$15.99 CDN

Throughout his many adventures in time and space,
the Doctor has encountered aliens, monsters, creatures
and demons from right across the universe. In this third
volume of alien monstrosities and dastardly villains,
Doctor Who expert and acclaimed author Justin Richards
describes some of the evils the Doctor has fought in
over forty years of time travel.

From the grotesque Abzorbaloff to the monstrous
Empress of the Racnoss, from giant maggots to the
Daleks of the secret Cult of Skaro, from the Destroyer
of Worlds to the ancient Beast itself… This book brings
together more of the terrifying enemies the Doctor has
battled against.

Illustrated throughout with stunning photographs and
design drawings from the current series of *Doctor Who*
and his previous 'classic' incarnations, this book is a
treat for friends of the Doctor whatever their age, and
whatever planet they come from…